Tokens of Promise

By Teresa Pollard

HopeSprings Books

©2013 by Teresa Pollard

All rights reserved. No portion of this book may be reproduced, stored in a retrieval system, or transmitted in any form or by any means—electronic, mechanical, photocopy, recording, scanning, or other—except for brief quotations in critical reviews or articles, without the prior written permission of the publisher.

Cover design by HopeSprings Books.
Cover art photo of "Shepherd's Staff"
©iStockphoto.com/milanklusacek

Published in the United States of America by HopeSprings Books, an imprint of Chalfont House Publishing.
www.HopeSpringsBooks.com
www.ChalfontHouse.com

Publisher's Note: This novel is a work of fiction. Although inspired by the characters and events in The Holy Bible, Genesis 38, names, characters, places, and incidents are either products of the author's imagination or used fictitiously.

ISBN 978-1-938708-14-5 (paperback)
ISBN 978-1-938708-18-3 (ebook)

Printed in the United States of America

To Wade,
Thank you for many wonderful years.

Author's Note
This is a work of fiction intended for mature eyes only.
All characters and events not taken from the Bible
or the Talmud are from the author's imagination.

TABLE OF CONTENTS

Book One

Chapter 1: page 1
Chapter 2: page 9
Chapter 3: page 23
Chapter 4: page 33
Chapter 5: page 53
Chapter 6: page 63
Chapter 7: page 71
Chapter 8: page 77
Chapter 9: page 87
Chapter 10: page 97
Chapter 11: page 103
Chapter 12: page 111
Chapter 13: page 117
Chapter 14: page 123

Book Two

Chapter 1: page 131
Chapter 2: page 139
Chapter 3: page 145
Chapter 4: page 155
Chapter 5: page 163
Chapter 6: page 171
Chapter 7: page 179
Chapter 8: page 185
Chapter 9: page 189
Chapter 10: page 195
Chapter 11: page 217

Glossary: **page 223**
Author's Notes: **page 223**
Discussion Guide: **page 231**
About the Author: **page 241**

Chapter 1

The blackness of the village well had him hypnotized when a scream ripped through the air. *Was that inside my head or in the village?* In slow motion, he struggled to his feet. His foot caught the edge of his cloak, and he nearly pitched into the deep hole, arms flailing. He regained his balance and his clumsy fingers fumbled to untie the leather girdle that gathered his cloak about his waist. The mate to his broken sandal, his knife, the water bags, and the bag of gold and silver nuggets that were in the fold of his cloak fell to the ground, forgotten as he scrambled up the stone steps. His loose tunic and bare feet were perfect for running, but as he reached level ground again, there was no clear indicator which direction he should run. No one was running anywhere. Perhaps he had imagined the scream after all. He began to turn to retrieve his possessions. No. Something was definitely wrong. People were staring at him. That was natural in the circumstances, but their eyes kept shifting away, some to the left, some to the ground. They had heard the cry. He was sure of it.

He heard the scream again and ran toward it. Others were following him now, though at a slower pace. He nearly tripped over the remains of a donkey, and he cursed both the town dwellers for their filthy paths and his own feet, which seemed determined to be his enemies. He had always considered himself as swift and surefooted as the jackals that plagued his sheep, but today he was as the lumbering bear tumbling from a rocky lair.

As the ramshackle houses became closer together, the people seemed more openly curious, and he had little trouble finding his way. Why was he compelled to answer the distress call? Apparently, no one else was concerned. He was a stranger here. It could not only be dangerous, it could be foolish.

Then the crowd thinned to reveal her. Her astounding beauty made him catch his breath. She could be little more than a girl, but already her body gave promise of delight in its soft curves. She lay nearly naked, her modesty retained only by the shiny black tresses that fell over her half-formed breasts and down to her thighs. She clutched at a pile of shredded garments that lay heaped about her feet, and sought to cover herself with them. Though finely embroidered, the garments were not the soft stuff one might expect of a harlot, but neither were they the coarse clothing of a slave.

She looked up at Judah. Her eyes reached out to him for assistance, but she spoke no words and her arms remained tightly clasped around the wisps of linen. She was clearly not a Canaanite. Her small oval face was naturally pale under the yellow and green powder she wore on her eyelids and cheeks. Even her cosmetics were not the bold painting of a harlot. She reminded him of Rachel, the beautiful wife of his father Jacob, whom Judah had loved for her gentleness. But Judah also despised Rachel because Jacob had loved her instead of his own mother, Leah.

The scene was suspended in time as he gawked in stunned silence at her deep brown eyes. Also frozen was a foul smelling but richly dressed man of Tyre. The shaft of the twisted carob staff he held poised over her body featured gold and lapis lazuli bands. A carved human head formed the handle at the top. As Judah's gaze met the glare of the slave trader, he burned with an instant hatred. *Be cautious now.* He was not usually an impetuous man. That was the curse of his brothers, Simeon and Levi. However, today the breeze had carried away his good sense like barley chaff.

"Stop!" Judah surprised even himself by shouting.

The man of Tyre lowered his weapon somewhat. The two men eyed each other like combatants in a wrestling contest, each sizing up the other for possible weaknesses. Judah was younger, and probably the stronger of the two, though he held no weapon. His short, loose tunic revealed his muscularity. The strong fingers of his large shepherd's hands had choked the life from a wolf attacking his ewes. Although the man of Tyre wore the long embroidered cloak and full sleeves of a man of leisure, his scarred face and agile stance belied any feebleness. Judah guessed him to be a pirate, one who ravaged the coastal towns and cities, plundering their goods and making slaves of their peoples. Such men were tolerated, and even respected, as wealthy merchants who brought much-needed goods into the countryside for sale to the people or as gifts to local kings. Foreign slaves were more valuable because they could be worked harder and given fewer rights than local-born slaves.

The man spat at Judah's feet. "Who are you, Hebrew, that you would dare to defy me, Ben Qara, a merchant in the service of King Hammurabi? Go away, or I will have your master whip you to the thirty-ninth lash. I may even pay him that he will make it forty."

Angered at first by Ben Qara's speech, Judah actually laughed when he realized that his bare feet and loose tunic had caused the man of Tyre to think him a slave. "I have no master but Yah, Ben Qara. I am Judah, the son of Jacob, Prince of Hebron."

The startled look on the slave trader's face made Judah smile. "Why do you abuse this child? What evil has she done to be so publicly humiliated? Do you not know that she is liable to stoning for appearing in the street in this manner?"

As Ben Qara picked up a fist-sized stone and tossed it to Judah, the young woman trembled with fear. "Perhaps you'd care for the honor of throwing the first one, Prince. She resists my attempts to make her my wife. Is it not my duty to beat her to submission? You evidently know the law. What do you say? Have I not the right?" His semi-toothless grin was triumphant as Judah's countenance fell. Judah dropped the stone.

"You have the right." Judah turned to the cowering girl with unfeigned compassion. "Why do you resist him, young woman? You are his wife. You are his to do with as he pleases. It is the law."

At first quietly, then with increasing confidence in his good will, she replied, "Is it truly the law, Kind Master? What kind of law is it that would condemn me to be stripped of my clothing and taken in the street like a common whore?"

As she tried to stand, she smothered a cry of pain and gripped the linen cloth to her breasts while she wrapped it around her blood-streaked back and buttocks.

"This man lied. He told my father, Benu'el, I was to be the bride of his younger son. I have many brothers and sisters, and my father required gold for his journey. Even so, he would never have sold me as a bride for this man. It is truly Yah that has brought you here this day, Master, for my father seeks your father in Hebron." She spat at the feet of Ben Qara.

Ben Qara lifted the staff to strike her again, but Judah stepped between them and averted the blow, catching the staff by its carved head and flinging it to the roof of a nearby hut. A couple of youngsters scrambled up to the roof to retrieve the valuable jeweled staff. Ben Qara would certainly be able to buy it back later if he cared to, though it would probably cost him royal weight.

Judah fended off Ben Qara's blows as if they plagued him no more than a locust on his ashcake might, and this seemed to unnerve the weaponless man of Tyre.

"You cannot believe the tales of this lying wench over my word. I am a wealthy merchant. I was able to pay the exorbitant bride price her father set. That was all he demanded of me." He lowered his fists and backed away.

Judah hesitated. "You deny then that you lied to the child's father?"

Of course, the innocent eyes could be lying to him to save her life, but somehow it didn't seem probable. The reputation of Benu'el of Chezib was far reaching, and here was this young woman claiming that her father had gone to seek Jacob. It had to be about him. Benu'el, the Man of God, had gone to tell Jacob that his son Judah had sold his own brother into slavery in Egypt and was now dead. It had to be. It was Yah's way of punishing him.

"Of course I deny it. I have no sons. My wife is barren. Why do you think I wanted this young one? She looks strong enough to give me many sons. Why else would I buy her?"

That he bothered to deny the claim at all somehow gave it even more weight. Most men dismissed the words of a woman as being of no more worth than the howl of a jackal. Judah was not most men. He knew that Ben Qara was less interested in the sons he could get by the beautiful female than in the pleasure he would have in getting them. "What will you take in payment for her? I will redeem her for her family. Then you may buy a young woman more willing to give you the sons you desire."

Ben Qara's snicker was crude. "For her family, is it now? Just what kin of hers are you? You don't look like her brother to me."

His greenish brown spit splattered the ground. Among his other vices, Ben Qara was seemingly addicted to chewing the bittersweet lupine grasses that grew in the steppe pasturelands. "Besides, you are a man of bare feet. What could you possibly have to give me in payment for this wicked but beautiful creature?"

"If she is who I believe her to be, I am indeed related to her, though admittedly with a distant relation. Never mind that. I can pay you whatever you demand, Ben Qara. If my belongings have not been stolen, they are in the well. Believe it or not, when I heard her cry, I was so possessed by the need to go help, I dropped everything without thought." He shook his head as though he had trouble believing his own story. "It does not matter. Even if my things are gone, my friend Hirah of Adullam will vouch for both my character and my wealth. You will get your money." He gave a half-nod of encouragement to the shaking girl. "What do you say, then? Will you allow me to redeem her?"

Grudgingly Ben Qara nodded his assent. "Her bride price was fifty shekels of silver, but she's yours for thirty. After all, as you said, she's damaged goods. The whole town has now looked upon her nakedness. Most she's good for now is a slave, and I'll wager she's not much good at that."

As both Judah and the girl recoiled from this final insult, Ben Qara kicked her leg. "Take her if you will, Prince of Hebron, but I prophesy that you will regret the day you ever met Tamar of Chezib. She is young, but her witching ways are strong. She is a dreamer who has grand notions about herself. Between her thighs lies disaster for the house of Judah."

"You talk foolishness, Ben Qara. I am redeeming her for her father, not myself. I have a wife, and sons as old as she is." The prophecy unnerved him, but he did not want to let the gaping crowd see that.

The smile on the trader's face was wide as he kept provoking, "Perhaps that is true, but it does not change the way you look at this Tamar. You desire her, and you cannot help yourself."

Judah glared at him. "I do not deny that you speak the truth, but lust is not love. Love is an act of the will, and I will not to love Tamar. I have a wife."

Chapter 2

Judah picked up his leather bag and shook out a handful of gold nuggets comparable to the weight of thirty silver shekels. "Here is your money, Ben Qara. I brought it as a gift to Benu'el of Chezib. I will give him back his daughter instead."

He tossed the hunks at the trader. Many of them fell to the ground around the well and rolled dangerously near the edge. Ben Qara scrambled to retrieve them. Turning his back, Judah put on his cloak and girdle and climbed the stone steps out of the well's pit.

"I have not weighed these, Hebrew. If some fall into the water, there may not be enough to buy the girl. You had best wait." He caught a chunk as it hit the edge.

Judah never looked back. "There were more than enough there. If you let them fall, I will not be responsible. You insisted on coming down here with me. The girl is mine now."

Although his words claimed her, Judah ignored Tamar as he returned down the narrow street toward the town gate. She had to run to keep pace with his long, determined stride.

"Kind Master, kind master," Tamar panted. "Won't you turn aside into my house? It is only around the corner."

"Do you mean that your family has not left yet?"

The anxiousness in his face seemed to startle her, and she spoke timidly. "No, Good Sir, I only meant that there is still food and my clothing there, and that you might refresh yourself from the heat of the sun."

He wavered. It was too hot to be traveling, but his earlier weariness was gone and he only wished to find the girl's father, the Man of God. He could buy her a garment in the marketplace on the way out of town. She must know that, but perhaps she was worried that she had already cost him too much. "I need to find the shoemaker before he leaves the bazaar. He has my broken sandal, and I promised to buy a new pair from him before I left town."

"I will send Joshua, a boy from the next house, to fetch Samuel the shoe merchant. He will come. Few of the people of our town can afford shoes. Besides, until we journey, which we seldom do, we have little need of them." She smiled.

Judah blinked. He had thought her bare feet were a result of her encounter with Ben Qara. Now he realized she had no shoes. Even the slaves in his household had shoes. But then, as tent dwellers who moved so often, it was necessary. The shoe merchant would be pleased this day. He would have at least two sales. Judah gestured for her to show him the way to her home.

The news of their meeting had spread to the street of her house before they arrived. People stared, some with friendly curiosity, and some glaring. Judah wondered what they thought. An old woman with thick white hair down to her feet came bustling from a hut somewhere at the end of the zigzag path. Small children tried to run to her with outstretched arms, but she absently shooed them back to their mothers. Her eyes fixed on Tamar, and Tamar flew to her like her littlest babe.

With Tamar enfolded in her tender embrace, she strode determinedly to Judah and demanded, "What do you intend to do with this child?"

"Nothing, Mistress." Judah somehow felt as guilty as when his mother had caught him and Dinah wrestling in the mud instead of swinging the butter churn. "I plan to restore her to her father as soon as possible."

The woman's face was downcast. "I doubt that he will take her back, young man. Old Benu'el is a good man, but he would not accept gladly the humiliation of this afternoon."

She lifted Tamar's face and wiped away tears with calloused but gentle hands. "Why did you resist the man, child? You have brought shame on your family."

"He was such an evil man, Grandmother Emi. He said he would use me until he grew tired of me and then sell me as a slave on one of his journeys. He said he would teach me to give him pleasure in ways that have not yet been dreamed of. I was so frightened." As her sobs grew more violent, the hastily wrapped pieces of her tunic slipped somewhat and revealed the welts of the dreadful beating she had taken.

Emi kissed Tamar's forehead and comforted her. "Of course you were, child. Do not worry. I will talk with your father."

She glared at Judah as if suddenly all men were abhorrent to her. He stared down at his feet. *Why do I feel like the culprit instead of the rescuer?* "If you are the girl's grandmother, I guess I can safely leave her with you and return to Adullam. From there I will send a message to her father asking him to return for her."

As he turned to leave, both women cried out, "No!", and then gasped that they had dared to command a man so loudly on a public street. Emi bowed her head and continued more quietly, "Tamar is legally yours now. I have no children, and yet I am mother to all the children of Chezib. I will not see this one hurt. You have redeemed her. Now you must make her your wife. Then her father will forgive her."

Stunned by the demand, Judah gawked, first at the old woman, then at Tamar, then at the curious neighbors who had long since ceased their labors to watch. Loudly, not sure whom he was addressing, he declared, "The girl needs no forgiveness. She has done no wrong."

Emi grunted. "A woman need do no wrong to need forgiveness from a man. It is the way of life."

Judah's head jerked back as if Yah's hand of truth had slapped him. So often, he had become angry with his wife, Ashuah, because of some problem he knew he himself had caused. "Yet I cannot make her my wife. I already have a wife."

The old woman shrugged. "What difference does that make? A man can have as many wives as he can afford, and certainly you can afford another." At his raised eyebrows, she explained. "Joshua saw your money in the well. It was his father, my brother, who protected it for you while you dealt with the trader."

"Then I must thank him. I am not generally so careless with my gold." Ben Qara had said Tamar was a witch. Perhaps he was right. "Nevertheless, I cannot marry her." He shook his head at her protests. "It is not a matter of money. I have vowed never to have but one wife, and I will not break that vow."

"Do you love your wife so much then?" The shrewd old woman's mouth pursed with disbelief. Judah stared at a few of the closer witnesses as though he could make them go away by just the strength of his will.

Emi bowed her head and asked permission to take Tamar into the house, cleanse her wounds, and help her change her garment.

He nodded consent. Why was it always so obvious that he cared so little for his wife? She was a Canaanite, and that was enough to make his father despise her, but that only made Judah more determined to care for her. They had been married many years now. She had been an excellent wife; they had two sons and a child soon to be born. Yet neither he, nor his father, was any closer to having real feelings for the poor woman. Ashuah was not beautiful, but she was far from ugly. Even with her body ripe with his children, she could still excite him. Her dark olive skin was ecstatic to his slightest touch, and her body swayed as she worked. Yet, were she to leave him, he knew that it would not matter in the least. The years they had shared were as nothing to him.

Perhaps that was the way it was with Jacob and Judah's mother. Leah had borne Jacob many sons; she could not repulse Jacob, though he often referred to her as the plain one. However, Rachel held all Jacob's love. She always had, her and her children. Joseph, the son of their love. The brother of his hatred, the brother he had sold as a slave. Sold to die in the land of Egypt.

"Will you not come into my home?" Tamar stood in the doorway of a mud-brick hut, a finely embroidered linen tunic wrapped around her thin body and fastened at the right shoulder with a tiny silver pin. Two large wooden combs held back her shining black hair. The old woman had done her work well in such a short time.

As he stepped into the room, he would have been safer walking into a bear's lair on the first day of spring. From the outside, the hut appeared as squalid as any of the others, but in here, it looked more like Eden. Someone had woven linen and wool dyed in red as deep as blood, and the blues of the sky, and the golds and grays of the desert sand into pictures that were only pictures in his mind. The fabrics that hung from the walls and lay on the floor were more magnificent than any he had seen in the bazaars on his travels with Hirah. Surely, Benu'el planned a speedy return to leave behind his treasures.

Shock made him speak bluntly. "I do not understand. How can you buy such cloth when you cannot afford shoes?"

Tamar tilted her head. "I did not say we were poor, Master, only that I have never had need of shoes because I have never been outside of the city gate. Moreover, we did not buy the cloth. Mother is a weaver. She taught me also when I was very small. Mother gives her cloth away. You may take whatever you will."

She moved to take down from the wall a piece he had been staring at, but he stayed her hand.

"We are not poor, Master. I have always had food; people bring us gifts of produce and even meat when they come to my father to settle their disputes and pray for their sicknesses. Until Father wished to journey, we had never had any need of anything else. Perhaps I could make you a cloak from this?" She held out a red, yellow, and purple striped cloth to him.

"No." He snatched the cloth from her hand and threw it to the floor. Wiping his eyes with his fingertips, he tried to calm himself. "You will have no time to make anything for me. I am taking you to your father at once."

"But first you must both have shoes," the old woman insisted. "The way to Hebron is steep and rocky. Let me get Joshua to run for Samuel for you."

"Such talk today of shoes! Of course we must have them. Send the boy for the merchant and leave me in peace." He sat on the floor beside the rumpled cloth and leaned his head against the wall. He ordered his body to relax, but the veins stood out on the hand that fingered the striped cloth.

While Emi was gone, Tamar stared at the reclining figure. He was such a big man, or so it seemed in the tiny room where he nearly stretched from one wall to the other. His curly brown beard was trimmed neatly to a point a palm's distance from his chin. Though closed now, his light brown eyes were like the land of Canaan with its cold snow-topped mountains in sight of the blistering wilderness. The sweat-glistening muscles he flexed when he was fighting Ben Qara were not so defined now, but he had no bulges of fat at his waist like most men of the town. The tiny wrinkles around his eyes and mouth lied if they led one to believe him old. What could have worried age into a face that could be so gentle? Yet it could also be harsh, as Ben Qara had cause to know.

"Will you have some wine while we wait, my Lord? My father's wine pot is not yet empty."

His eyelids remained closed. "I do not thirst yet. Tell me, young Tamar, have you weak eyes?"

"No, of course not, my Lord. My sight is very good. You need not worry that I would stumble on the mountain rocks. I am exceedingly surefooted."

The grim line of his mouth did not change as he muttered, "So you would be. You are too much like her for it to be otherwise."

She did not understand this remark, but she knew it to be somehow not to her benefit. A tiny cry escaped her lips as she slid down to a sitting position against the wall near his feet. The squeak sounded loud to her ears, like the bazaar on market day. Afraid that she might have angered him, she sat with her fingers intertwined at her ankles while her teeth bit into the flesh of her knees. She stared at his dark eyelashes. Her *go'el*, her redeemer. Who was this man who had saved her from the life of horror she could not quite imagine, but who now did not want her? He had admitted that he desired her, but desire was not enough for him.

Tamar had never before felt desire. Yet she recognized it in his eyes, and the beginnings of it stirred within her like an itching that would not go away and only this man could sooth it with his touch. The physical pain that had tortured her only a short time ago was already subsiding, replaced with a gentle pain that invited her to touch and kiss his prone figure. He had said he willed not to love her. She willed that he would.

They were still sitting in this manner when Emi returned. "Samuel is on his way. I have brought you both some food. You must be famished. I had no meat, but I brought fresh lentil soup, barley cakes, and cheese."

As Emi loosened the cord from the wool bag, she spread it open on the floor as a table for the feast. The bag also contained figs, almonds, olives and dates. The pleasant aroma from the clay pot of lentil soup made Tamar realize how long it had been since she had eaten. Yet if they ate all this, Emi might not have anything to eat for a while.

"Tamar, would you be a good child and come outside and comb my hair for me while our guest eats? No one can untangle it the way you do."

As Tamar tried to rise, her yelp reminded the older woman, "I have brought some garlic to rub on your back."

Immediately the Master jumped to his feet. Evidently, he was familiar with both the remedy and the incantation to Baal that usually accompanied it. "No! You will take a shekel and find some balm for her back. While her father is gone, I am in charge, and there will be no prayers said to anyone but Yah over her."

Emi was calm. "I had no thought of praying to anyone but Yah, Master. If you desire, I will buy balm, but the garlic is a good cure even without the prayers the Canaanites use."

As Emi led Tamar outside, Judah put the shekel back in his bag. He watched them for a while through the doorway as the girl ran the comb slowly down the length of Emi's white tresses. Though he couldn't make out the words, he saw the old woman speaking to her. Slowly and quietly she spoke. The surprised expression on the girl's face made him intensely curious.

He ate his meal in silence, glancing at the two women often, despite his efforts not to do so. As he finished eating, carefully saving large portions for the women, he made as much noise as possible so that they might know he was through and they could come in to eat. He decided to send his son Er back here with a goat kid and an *ephah* of barley to repay Emi. He raised the wineskin to his mouth. In the past several years, he had begun drinking more wine than was good for him. The wine helped to drown out his guilt over Joseph, but the guilt always resurfaced like a swimmer in the Salt Sea.

When the women came in and began quietly eating, a strange familiarity in the scene struck him. Years ago, he had run away from home because he could not stand to look into his father's eyes and know that his father wished it were he who had been killed instead of Joseph. What his father did not know was that Judah wished it also. In the town of Adullam, life had been riotous because it was harvest time. The Canaanites and the followers of Yah were all feasting. The heathens were reveling in praise of their god, Baal, while those who called on the name of Yah were giving thanks in a more subdued manner. Though Judah was staying with his friend Hirah, he had wandered out to observe the festivities. The chaos was quickly overwhelming to a man more accustomed to the peace of herding sheep. When Shua, a Canaanite woman, offered him the hospitality of her relatively quiet home, he had gratefully escaped the town's noise. Shua's daughter served him dinner and wine, and then more wine. When he awakened in the morning, he found that he had a wife, and another sin to confess to his father. He had hoped that when Er was born Father Jacob might relent and bless the boy, but he had not.

The vision was so strong; he jolted from his reverie as from a nightmare. Here he was, again in town during a time of celebration, the end of the spring lambing season, enjoying a feast in a home with an unmarried woman. He tossed aside the wineskin. "No, we will not wait any longer for the shoe merchant. We will find him on our way out of town."

"You need not find me. I am here." The man Judah had met upon entering Chezib stood in the opening holding Judah's repaired sandal as well as an identical new pair of sandals in his right hand and a much smaller pair of leather boots in his left.

"Come in, Samuel," the old woman invited. "Let me get this food out of the way so that you can show our guest your shoes."

"Sandals are sandals. I have no need to see. Just be sure that those boots fit the girl's foot." He was immediately sorry for his gruff voice. The law of hospitality was one of the first things he had learned at his father's knee. He softened his tone, "Please be as quick about it as possible. The girl and I are in a hurry to leave."

The old man rubbed his graying beard and spoke with a puzzled frown. "But I had been given to understand that you arrived in Chezib on foot?"

"So. That is true, but what does it matter?"

Samuel bowed before him. "Forgive me for being an inquisitive old man, Master. I only wondered what could be so important that a son of Abraham would risk the robbers and wild animals by rushing onto the road at nightfall."

The girl was not used to travel, so they would barely be out of sight of the city before the sun set. The old woman had not forgotten. She had delayed them. Now that Judah knew they would not be leaving, he was anxious to play host.

"Forgive me, my friend, my haste not only covered my eyes to the time of day, but to my lack of hospitality concerning you. Will you not join me in a little wine to celebrate the end of lambing season? Do I understand that you are also of the *Habiri* tribe, Samuel?"

Samuel nodded his head vigorously as he laid the shoes at Judah's feet and sat down against the wall facing him and the women. "Yes, my brother. I am the son of Jerah, the son of Joktan, the son of Eber, the son of Shem. Benu'el is my cousin." He bowed his face to the floor. "I thank you in his name for your act of bravery this day."

Samuel caressed the soft leather of the boots. "I measured your new sandals to the size of the broken one, so you are assured of a good fit. Although I repaired the old one as best I could, it is extremely old, and I cannot guarantee how long it will last before it breaks again as it did today."

Judah didn't wish to pursue the subject of his shoe. Though he had blamed the sandal-breaking accident on a rock, the truth was the shoes had been repaired many times. The price of a brother: a pair of shoes. "What about the boots for the girl?"

"Her father had me make them a few days ago." At her gasp of surprise, he held his hands up. "All he said was that you would be traveling soon after your wedding. Now that my business is concluded, I will have that wine, Emi."

"Your business is not quite concluded, cousin," Judah said, weighing two of his larger nuggets in his left hand. "Here, I believe these should be enough. Now, let us drink."

As he also felt the weight of the gold in his palm, Samuel smiled and nodded. Tamar dipped wine from the pot in the corner and handed the crockery bowl to Emi who gave it to Judah to serve his guest.

"Since you are her cousin, Samuel, then I may safely leave the girl with you. By myself, I might be able to catch up with her father before daybreak."

Samuel shook his head with a dismayed expression. "I am so sorry, my friend. I have such a large family that we hardly have room to sleep. I had hoped to buy a slave today that could help me to build a larger house. But I could not afford it." He grasped Judah's wrist. "Do not worry so. I have already sent a messenger after Benu'el. He will be back here as soon as possible. However, I fear you must be resolved. If I know my cousin, and trust me I do, he will insist that you marry his daughter."

Chapter 3

It was the blackness of the night. The master had not been able to persuade Samuel to stay. Emi was either asleep in the corner or giving a very good imitation of it. Not a sound was coming from the part of the floor where the big man lay. Tamar was restless. She tried not to make a sound, but she was not comfortable in any position, and every movement pained her. Following Emi's instructions, she rose and unfastened her garment. The linen clung to her back, however, so it would not fall to the floor. She held it until she lay beside Judah then spread it open. She reached her hand out to touch him. A larger, more muscular hand grabbed her, and his other hand stifled her scream.

"So, Ben Qara was right. You are a witch, young Tamar. Did you think to so easily win yourself a man?"

Tears blinked in her eyes as she nodded. As he took his hand away, she whispered, "I am sorry, Master. Emi said that if I lay beside you naked and touched you in that place, you would flame with desire and not be able to help yourself."

His anger seemed to melt from his face as she spoke. "Well, she was at least half right. A little more wine, and she might have won. But it takes a great deal of wine to make a man who has drunk as much as I have in the last few years lose his senses."

He lay on his side and propped his head with his forearm. "Cover yourself up, Little One. We will talk this night away. I dare not sleep again in your presence. You may tell the old woman that her plan might have worked were it not for her garlic remedy. You cannot sneak up on a man when your aroma comes before you so strongly."

She could not help laughing at this, and he smiled in response.

"Tell me of your life, Master. What is it like in the great city of Hebron? Have you a palace there?" She turned to her stomach and laid her chin in her fists. The master must have marvelous tales of miracles and wonders of jewel-studded wagon wheels that trod the gold-paved streets.

"It is good that your plan did not work for you, Little One, if that is what you desire. My people live in tents in the pasturelands surrounding Hebron. I abhor the life of the city, as did my fathers before me. My great-grandfather Abraham once lived in the great Chaldean city of Ur, but he was pleased to come here to the land that Yah had promised him. Ur was a wicked city, but he did learn there the greatest skill that a man can learn. He learned to write; to put his thoughts in clay that men he has never met may know them, and send their own thoughts back to him."

Tamar had heard of this skill, though she had never seen it, but she wished him to tell her of it. She liked hearing the loving tone of his voice. She nodded encouragingly.

"The people in that city use the skill mostly for business. But think of the possibilities, Little One. I could write for my children's children the events of the lives of their grandfather's father. That way the story is preserved from generation to generation and not lost or distorted in the telling. Is that not the most wonderful thing a man might learn?"

"Yes, my Lord, it is." She couldn't keep the enthusiasm out of her voice. "Have you this ability, Master?"

Even in the darkness, she could feel the expression change on his face as his voice softened. "No, child, I have not. Abraham taught the skill to his son Isaac and Isaac to his son, my father, Jacob. However, Jacob had twelve sons, and he taught the skill to only one, my brother Joseph. The rest of us were shepherds, and what need have shepherds to write their thoughts?"

"But Master, could you not convince your father?"

He shook his head. "I was born to the wrong mother. My father had two wives: Leah, my mother, and Rachel, her sister. *Abba* Jacob loved Rachel with a love that consumed him. He worked for my grandfather Laban for fourteen years to win her for himself. He should have had her in the seventh year, but Grandfather cheated him by giving him my mother Leah instead so that Jacob might remain and manage his estate for him. Father was clever and the hand of Yah was with all that he did, which was making my grandfather rich indeed. Anyway, for many years Rachel was barren. She and my mother also gave Jacob their maids that they might bear children in their names. Then Joseph was born to Rachel, and it was as though he had no need of any other child but the son of their love." Judah rumpled her hair in the darkness. "Do you not see, Little One? That is why I cannot marry you. You are so much like Rachel; so beautiful to behold, and with a laugh that brings joy to my bones just to hear it. I have two sons now, and another child soon to be born. I cannot do to them what my father did to me. And I would. I know it. A child in your belly would fill me with such delight that I would forget everyone else. Can you understand that?"

She nodded and pulled the hand on her head around to kiss it. "But what of the skill, Master? Can you not get your brother to teach it to you?"

"I only wish that I could, Little One." He patted her cheek before he drew his hand away. "I have done a very evil thing, young Tamar; a thing that makes a man like Ben Qara look like a righteous man. At least the men he sells as slaves are strangers, captured in some semblance of a battle. I made a slave of my own brother, foolishly selling him to a man much like Ben Qara."

Why he told her, she would never know, never understand, but she would not believe his words. "I cannot believe that, Master."

"Nevertheless, it is the truth. Now you can be glad I am not to be your husband. Who could want such an evil man?"

"Tell me how it happened, Master," she whispered. No matter how often he repeated it, she could never believe him evil.

"I was young at the time, though that is no excuse. My brothers and I were out in the fields as usual. We worked hard; harder than any of the slaves or hirelings worked, but nothing was ever good enough to please my father. He constantly accused us of going off and leaving the sheep unattended to spend time riotously in town. Occasionally one or the other of my brothers did go off for a while, but they never neglected his sheep. Never. We all loved him too much. But he couldn't see that. Anyway, as I said before, I hate towns, so I never went anywhere but to the top of the mountain to try to write in the dirt. Joseph found me there one day and laughed at my crude efforts. He was always spying on us and boasting before Father. Until that day, I had always protected him from my brothers for my father's sake. But not after that. After that, I hated him with ten times their hatred."

His fist clenched, and Tamar stroked it. "Like you, he was a dreamer of dreams, and he said he was going to be a king or something and we would all have to bow down to him. Father had given him the long-sleeved coat of a man of leisure. It was of a cloth very much like this one your mother made, and it was to be the mark of a scholar. He was not to be a shepherd like the rest of us. He would be taught the skills of reading and writing that I had begged Father to teach me for years.

"Up in the hills in Dothan one day, we saw Joseph coming in the distance. We were all hot, tired, and hungry, and the sight of that coat enraged us. He was sure to go back and make a big fuss to Father because we were at Dothan instead of at Shechem as we had planned; never mind that the grass at

Shechem was not a finger's width long at the time. We were convinced he would make up some wild explanation and Father would believe him, as usual. When Levi suggested we kill him, he did not really mean it at first, I don't think, but the idea gripped me with such intensity, I truly believe I could have done it with my bare hands. I hated him that much. Reuben stopped us, though I'll never understand why. He was just as angry as the rest of us were, but he convinced the others to put Joseph down into a pit and let the wild animals eat him. Later, when we had all calmed down, Reuben was planning to rescue him. In the meantime, he had to go back up to the top of the mountain to check on the sheep, and while he was gone I saw a caravan coming, and I talked my brothers into selling Joseph to the slave traders who were headed to Egypt."

"See. I knew you were not evil. You saved your brother's life."

He snorted. "Hardly. You do not know what life is like for a slave in Egypt. It would have been kinder had I killed him quickly. We slaughtered a goat and poured its blood on the cloak so that Father would think a wild beast had killed Joseph, and at first that was exactly what he did believe. Later though, I think I was acting so guilty that he decided I had killed Joseph and my brothers were lying to protect me. In a way, I guess he was right. I've traveled to Egypt several times to find Joseph, and I have sent messengers at least once a year. We even traced Joseph to Pharaoh's prison, but he has never been heard from since. He isn't in the prison anymore. That much I know. Men die in those prisons, or they are hanged to suit Pharaoh's pleasure. I don't know which happened to Joseph." His left hand clutched the striped cloth, and he brought it to his face. "Dreams die with their dreamers, Young Tamar. Remember that."

"No, Master. I cannot. I do not believe that your brother is dead. Nor are his dreams. My father went to Hebron to give your father a message of hope. Had he only consolation, he would have remained here, for you are the one who needs it." She moved closer to him, and held him as though he was a child and his life depended on her rocking him through his sickness.

For many hours, they lay that way together, neither one speaking a word, but not sleeping, only staring into the darkness. Finally, in the pre-dawn, he stirred and turned toward her. Carefully he moved aside the embroidered linen and ran his hand down her soft pale skin. "I will not hurt you, my beautiful young wife. Do you trust me?"

She nodded and he moved to slide upon her without putting any weight down and hurting her already battered body.

"Master Judah, are you here? Master Judah?"

The voice in the dim gray outside the doorway halted his action immediately, and he pulled the linen back over her and jumped to his feet. An outline of a figure was barely visible.

"Is that you, Oni? What are you doing here, and how did you find me in the middle of the night?"

The grinning face of Joshua peeping from behind the servant's cloak answered that question. Joshua had had such an exciting day; he must have slipped out of his house in the night to see if the morning would bring any more fortune to his path. It seemed it had, for he shouted joyfully as the servant slipped him something and he ran away.

"Is there something wrong at Adullam? Has Hirah been hurt?" Judah strode to the doorway, asking his questions as he went. In the darkness, Tamar resumed her place at the opposite wall and refastened her garment.

The scuffling noises and the high pitch of the Master's voice indicated that something was happening here and he had interrupted. He hastened to apologize. "Yes, Master, it is I, Oni. I am sorry to have disturbed your sleep. Nothing is wrong at Adullam, but we have had word from the camp that you have another son, and Mistress Ashuah has named him Shelah. We thought you would want to know as soon as possible."

Hirah had thought so or at least he was so worried about his friend that he had insisted someone come here to give him the news, and Oni had obeyed in spite of a feeling that his Master would not welcome an interruption to his visit with the Man of God.

Judah gave him a reassuring slap on the back. "Do not be a fool, Oni. Come in and get some rest. You have brought good news. Why should I be angry? We will have wine to celebrate. Tamar, can you get my faithful servant wine in the darkness, or shall we light the lamp?"

Oni stepped around the old woman who sat up and stared at him. In spite of his words, Master Judah was acting nervous and angry for some reason. Oni had known all of Jacob's children since they were born, and the boys had never been able to fool him. He had known about the incident with Joseph from the beginning. Their guilt had been obvious to him, and they had confessed. Twice he had been sent to Egypt to find Joseph. He loved Judah as his own son, but he had no use at all for that little sneak, Joseph. But what was going on here? The bounce in the boy's step was due to more than the birth of another son. He was sure of it. And when the girl lit the clay lamp and stood silhouetted in its flame, he thought he knew the cause. Love had caught the boy in its net at last.

"How is it with your family, Oni?" Judah asked.

"It is well, Master. Deborah sends her respect." He hesitated, and then delivered the rest of her message. "She wishes to know, Sir, when we might announce the marriage of our daughter Ruah to your son Er?"

Judah bit into his thumb as he had often done as a child when he was about to say something that angered his father. "I cannot do that, Oni. If Benu'el will give permission, Er will instead be married to Tamar as soon as possible."

A crockery wine bowl fell to the floor and shattered into many pieces.

Chapter 4

Judah lay in a half sleep through the entire morning, knowing he was safe from any more women's trickery as long as Oni was present. The expression on the faithful old man's face when he had told him Er was to marry Tamar grieved him. It had been understood between them for years that Ruah and Er would marry when they were old enough. Part of the bride price would be Oni and Deborah's freedom. He had never actually placed Oni's hand on his thigh in pledge of it; it was an unspoken knowledge. It was not proper for a man to be slave to his daughter's father-in-law. Perhaps he should offer to give Oni his freedom anyway, but he would probably not accept it. He would pin his ear to the doorpost and become ever more a bond slave. He wished Oni had uttered some word of rebuke, as he had when Judah was a child and had provoked him past tolerance. However, he was not a child any more, and Oni could not rebuke him as he deserved.

Deborah would not dare to speak her anger to Judah directly, but poor Oni would bear the edge of her wrathful tongue for weeks. Ashuah was not going to be happy with the news either, so he had better prepare his stomach for a long siege of overcooked or badly seasoned lentils. He determined not to think of the beauty of Tamar and what might have happened if Oni had not come, but he could think of little else.

*Her long hair falls away
from her breasts like fleece
before the shearer.*

*The sweat of her maidenhair
as the morning dew in
the fertile valley.*

*Her smell of garlic,
which yet makes me smile,
an incense lifted to Yah.*

*The little cry she made
as she sat down so quietly
at my feet like a lamb caught*

*in the thorns that needed
a shepherd to caress
away its pain.*

Tokens of Promise

*My lips feel dry as desert
rocks. I lick them to no avail.*

As he awakened fully to the midday sun in his eyes, Judah jumped up and strode through the village's alleyways to find solitude. He wished not only to rid himself of the night's wine, which he blamed for the pain in his groin, but also to find the peace in his spirit that had eluded him for such a long time. He had found it last night for a few moments, but it had been snatched from him again like a mother's nipple from her babe. Why did he not break the oath he had made so often since childhood? He could not. Though he desired Tamar as a second wife with all his heart, he just could not.

When he returned to Benu'el's home and put on his cloak and sandals, he stood before the doorway with his hands raised to the heavens and prayed in a loud chanting voice, "Praise be to You, O Yah, our God, Ruler of the universe, who made..."

As he stood there with his arms raised like a terebinth tree, Tamar was unable to turn away. Her *go'el* looked so like a household god, that it seemed strange to know that he also worshipped a God: her God, Yah. Yesterday she had been a child, but in the night, Yah in his wisdom had made her a woman in her heart if not in her body. This man had called her his wife, and though he now wished to deny that and give her to his son, surely her father would not allow it. She had lain before the Master naked, and he had been so close to coming in to her that she had felt him touch her leg. When Ben Qara had tried to come near to her, she had been terrified, but the gentle voice of Judah was a balm that soothed away fear. She had wanted to be his wife. She did yet. She prayed that Yah in his wisdom would one day make it so.

Tamar had been busy since the dawn. Emi had returned to her own home to prepare for the spring celebration with her brother's family. Tamar had already trimmed the wick of the clay lamp and hung it beside the doorway on its heavy goat hair cord, gone to the well to draw water several times that her guests might wash when they were ready, and laid out food for them. There was this day plenty of food. Her friends had this morning pressed many offerings for Father Benu'el into her hands. She was hungry, but it was forbidden that she eat before Judah did.

She had never realized how much work her mother would have to do if she did not help. Now she was a wife, at least in her own heart, and the chores were a labor of love. However, that did not make the work easy. Her back throbbed, and she walked with slight grace, bumping every obstacle in her path. She was tired; the day seemed to be passing far too slowly, and she was eager for her father to return.

Her *go'el* certainly spoke many long prayers. Just as she was passing Judah in the doorway, a rumble from his stomach made her smile. He quickly closed his prayer, stepped inside and sat to be served. He began to pray again, "Praise be to You, O Yah, Who makes bread to come forth from the earth...", but this time his prayer was fairly short, and Tamar finished up the meal preparations.

Father was going to be angry with her. As she pondered, Tamar stirred the dark brown lentil beans and dipped them into the wooden bowls. Maybe he would not. Maybe he would know that her destiny was with this man. It seemed that Father had some idea. He had had Samuel make her shoes. She rubbed the soft kid boots that felt so strange against her calves. Why had he not mentioned them to Ben Qara unless he knew he was not the man with whom she would be traveling? In addition, he had left the wine vat almost half-full, so he must have known someone would be coming back to the house. She would soon be a wife, she was sure. It was not long before Judah and Oni were fed and Tamar could sit down to eat.

For many months, Judah had looked forward to the end of the time when the lambing so he could leave Hebron and come to Chezib to find Benu'el. He had thought of little else, though he had told only Oni and Hirah of his true intent. His family knew he had many business dealings with Hirah, and they thought him there in Adullam. He had left Oni there to await his return. To see the Man of God and confess his guilt had been such an overwhelming passion. Now he had little wish to see him.

If he could not convince Benu'el to let Tamar marry his son Er, what would he do? He would not see her disgraced for his own indecision. He would marry her. No, it must not be. Perhaps they should leave before the old man returned. No, that must not be either. He must face this. If only he could do so without the knowledge that he had himself uncovered her in the night. She was so soft and her small arms around his neck were so tender. He was a fool.

He looked over at the old woman dipping her bread into the garlic broth, and wondered if she had truly been asleep. The snores coming rhythmically from her pallet had seemed genuine enough, but even if she were asleep, he felt she somehow knew his secret. Not that Tamar would have told her; she would be the keeper of his secrets to her deathbed. It was the old woman herself. She was either a prophetess or a witch. He was not certain which. He feared her. If she spoke her knowledge to old Benu'el …

The next day, Benu'el returned with the setting sun. Emi sat by the fire warming her old bones and shelling brown lentil pods for another pot of stew. Old Benu'el and the determined young Master were deep in discussion. Tamar's mother had taken the girl to Emi's house so they could confer privately and leave the men to their conversation. Children ran foot races and tossed stones for distance further up the street. Only an old woman could be considered unimportant enough to be allowed to remain within hearing, and by the looks he cast toward her, the young Master didn't approve, but apparently he didn't want to offend Old Benu'el by demanding her dismissal.

Old age had betrayed her two nights previous. Falling asleep just when her baby needed her. Something important had happened between them, sure as seedtime, to bring that guilty look on the young Master's face every time he looked at her, or rather didn't. Just like Joshua when he took one of the raisin cakes without asking. However, Tamar had shaken her head dejectedly when asked if he had come in to her, and the child would never lie to her, not about that. Indeed, Tamar's truthfulness had gotten her into more trouble in her life than lying. People just didn't always want to hear the truth of a matter.

The young Master was fidgeting. He talked circles around the reason that Benu'el was on his way to Hebron, but he failed to ask straight out and old Benu'el didn't play the game in response. Something to remember there. When were they going to get around to the child? Men and their talk. Why could they not ever say what they meant plain-like, without all the speeches?

Ah, now they were at it. The honey-dipped words were gone. Benu'el trembled and shook his bony old finger at the young Master while he shouted in his deep "Thus says Yah" voice that usually sent mature men running to do his bidding like beardless young boys. His face was so red beneath his scraggly gray beard that she feared for him. Such anger wasn't good for an old man. But the young Master's face was almost purple. Up and down the small room he paced as he threatened and cajoled; his agile tongue hammering on Benu'el's one great weakness, Yah forgive an old man, his foolish pride.

On his way toward Adullam at last, Judah exhaled with relief. Old Benu'el hadn't been half so hard to convince as he had been led to suppose. He had given in to his persuasions with hardly a quibble. Oh, a few dire warnings, but what else could one expect of an old man? There were a few dreadful moments, though, when he hadn't seemed an old man at all. His eyes had looked through Judah, and they were sharp, sharp as Cain's dagger. Nevertheless, he had consented, and that was all that was important, wasn't it?

Perhaps Benu'el was afraid of the scandal if Tamar were left behind as Judah had threatened. Not that he really would do it. He couldn't even if he wanted to. He couldn't leave those trusting eyes to face the wicked tongues of the town gossips. His way, Benu'el could just say she had gone off to be married. He would not have to tell them it was not to the man who had spent the night in her home.

Had it been only three days since he had journeyed this road? He kept stealing furtive glances back at Tamar, who was almost running to keep up with his determined strides, and Oni, trailing slowly far behind her. She had been truthful; she had a natural grace that measured distances to rocks and compensated for them so that she never seemed to misstep.

Her town garment was too long for travel. He would take a knife to it when they reached Adullam. That would be much better than her continuing to lift it as she ran. *Won't Hirah be surprised?* Judah had gone to Chezib to find freedom, and had found instead a daughter-in-law. Better that, at least, than a wife. What had made him so foolish as to tell her his secret? True, he had gone to Chezib to tell the Man of God, but why her? Could he not wait for Benu'el to arrive before purging himself of the filth of it without burdening her?

"Goodbye, my friend. May your Yah bless your steps through your journey, and bring you safely to your tents." Hirah embraced Judah in his mighty arms and took the breath from him. Next to the tiny Tamar, Hirah appeared even more a giant, but Judah knew that in the days it had taken him to gather his supply caravan together, the giant's heart had been slain by the girl's innocent bewitchment.

Hirah now turned to her and spoke with a conspiratorial tone. "Well, if I cannot convince you to leave my friend and stay here with me, I have a gift for you, Little One, to take to Hebron. My trading partner may be angry with me for the extra trouble it is to carry the thing, but you need not worry about that."

As Hirah and Tamar made a great many bows to each other, Judah bowed also from his laughter. "What have you bought that could anger me, my friend?" he asked between gasps.

"Wait 'til you see." When Hirah clapped his hands, five slaves arrived carrying on their shoulders a large black bowl of at least four great cubits across with another bowl of almost equal size inverted on top of it. The slaves staggered under the great weight as they lowered it to the ground in front of the three of them. At Hirah's nod, they hurried away.

"Yah, be merciful, Hirah!" Judah exclaimed. "What could the best of wives want with iron bowls that size? You have surely been caught by the double scaled merchant this time." While Oni and the two men were again filling the air with the sounds of their mirth, Tamar attempted to lift the top bowl and examine its mysteries.

"What is it, Master Hirah?" Her eyes were wide with wonder.

The giant man squatted beside her. "It is an oven, girl. You have this foolish old grandfather here bury the bottom bowl in the ground and build a fire in it. Then you lay this flat piece over and put your food on it. With this bowl down on top of it, you soon have delicious cakes without an awful ash taste to them at all."

When Hirah lifted the top piece again, the girl became so engrossed in examining the thing that Judah feared she would someday be caught in it and burned. Judah also squatted beside the new cooking device. "But my friend," he protested, "I have only eight donkeys and two ox-pulled wagons with me on this trip, and they are loaded down with every *qerah* they can carry. We ourselves will have to walk the entire journey. Even without this, it will take us at least two weeks, but if my

Tokens of Promise 43

servants have to carry this, only Yah knows how long it will take us."

"You are only jealous, my friend, because you will still have to eat ashes while your son enjoys the delicacies of the little princess." Hirah slapped his shoulder. "I will send my own wagon and a team of oxen to carry my gift. It should not slow you down more than a day or two. Your wife has just had a child so it cannot be that one more day is any great burden, is it my friend?"

As Hirah's palm again greeted Judah's back, tears came to Judah's eyes, and he had to catch his breath again; one of the difficulties of having such a mighty friend.

When they crested the first hill on their journey homeward, he looked back to see Hirah still standing at the entrance to his great house. The painted masonry was far superior to even the best in Chezib, and the inner courtyards and enormous rooms would bear up to comparison with any in Hebron or Bethel. Yet in the midst of his wealth, and amid myriads of servants and even concubines, Hirah, like Jacob, was a lonely man. They had much in common, were they not both too stubborn to *admit* it.

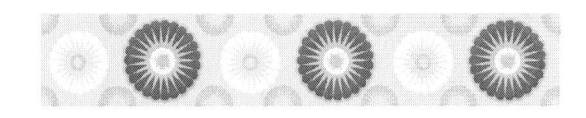

Tamar seemed delighted by the openness of the hill country. She ran ahead of the caravan to the top of every knoll and stared out into the distance before turning back to wave at him as he trudged beside the ox cart steadying the wretched oven. Finally, he called Enoch, one of his younger servants, to guard the bowls while he took charge of a donkey, freeing him to shadow Tamar. Not that there was much danger. Most wild animals would keep their distance even from a caravan this small. Yet he worried about her when she ran ahead in her eagerness to see the landscape, seeming to print in her mind every detail of light and color. Although, all there was to see was another valley leading to another hill. One hill after another with the valleys ever smaller between. Rocks piled upon rocks to form altars or simply to build campfires were the only signs that others had passed this way many times before. Yet at each crest, the girl stood enraptured as if the vista before her were a vision of loveliness such as she had never seen before. Indeed the hills did seem unusually full of wildflowers growing between the stones. She picked handfuls as she came to them and she braided garlands to put in her hair and around her neck. As he paused to have a drink, she even caught him by surprise and looped a garland about his neck. Oni's laughter was kind enough and Judah left it there a while before committing it to his bag.

"How did you meet Master Hirah, Master? I mean, you seem such different men, though both full of goodness. I mean..."

Judah looked up at her from a rock in the shade of a large carob tree where they rested from the heat of the midday sun. He offered her the wineskin. "Would you uncover all of my family secrets, Little One?"

He tossed a rock at a distant fig tree, which dropped a small branch loaded with figs. She walked slowly behind as he hastened over to retrieve them. He held up his hands as she began to apologize. "You might as well know. It is no real secret anyway, and you would hear it sooner or later."

He waited, however, until they had returned to the shade of the carob to begin. "My brothers Simeon and Levi avenged the dishonor of my sister, Dinah, by Shechem the Hivite by destroying almost an entire city. However, Shechem and his father, Hamor, had other family and friends outside the city who declared the law of blood revenge against our family. One day while tending my sheep near Dothan, I fell into the hands of five of those relatives. Praise Yah, it happened that Hirah was passing through on one of his many buying excursions, and he took my welfare as his *mitzvah* of the day. With all good speed they ran from the fury of his powerful fists."

The sweet fig he handed her halted her questions for the moment, and he led them back to the caravan. But her questions were not yet at an end. She came up to him as he shifted the load on his donkey.

"Master, I wondered if perhaps you might send back to the city of Ur to find a slave to teach your family the wonderful art of writing?"

He didn't at first hear her words. When she repeated her inquiry, he laid his head on the pile of bags on the donkey's back. "I have made my sons to be shepherds as I was, my child. It is too late to change that now."

"Why is that, my Lord? Is a man ever too old to learn? Can a shepherd not also be a man of learning?"

Judah wasn't sure how to answer. Could it be that he was not yet too old to fulfill the desire of his heart? It was worth considering. Already the girl knew him too well. "You are wise far beyond your years, Little One."

He hesitated. His eyes met hers briefly. "I will think on what you have said. Run off now and enjoy your wildflowers. It gives me joy to watch your youthful exuberance."

As the days passed, Tamar grew wearier with each step. She had had so little sleep this week. Why had her father let her down so? First, he gave her to that smelly old man to be attacked and beaten. But Father was a prophet. How had he not known that Ben Qara had no son? Now she was being sent away again to be a bride to a son she had never met. She lifted her eyes to the southern hills towards Hebron, the land of Judah, the land of Er. What would her new husband be like?

Er sat on a large rock and amused himself by throwing pebbles at the sheep grazing on the side of the hill. He hated sheep herding. His father was a rich man; why should he not have a hireling to do this for him? He should be a man of leisure and have fine clothing and women. Many women to wait on him and grant his every desire.

"Er, where are you?"

He stood and waved to Ruah. He liked watching her wade through the waves of sheep. She always raised her arms high above her head, and her full breasts bounced. In a few years, they would sag, and they would no longer excite him, but for now she was shapely if a little too round.

As she reached him, her words came out in spurts while her bosom heaved for breath. "A messenger came...from your father...bringing you a wife."

He yanked her down onto the rock beside him. "What is this? A wife for me? Where is she? Is she beautiful?"

Tears streamed down Ruah's cheeks, and she buried her face in her hands. They were such ugly hands, he had always thought, but then, the rest of her was so tempting that he could forgive the hands. However, he was impatient to learn of his wife, and he couldn't understand her words for the sobs. "Ruah, my Dove, where is this messenger with my bride?"

His calm voice worked its effect well enough as he lifted her chin in his palm.

"Back at the tents being given wine and wheat cakes by my Mistress, your Mother." She gulped, and he bade her to go on. "But your wife will not arrive for three days. She travels with our fathers and the servants and goods your father purchased on his journey."

"Why are they taking so long?" Er interrupted.

Ruah shrugged. "It seems your father was quite successful and has much to bring."

"What does she look like? Did the messenger say?" He could hardly contain his curiosity.

Ruah shook her head.

He gazed at her intently. "Why are you so upset? You will still be my wife also. I will have two wives. My father must know I am going to be a very rich man and will have need of them."

In a gesture meant to be tender, he pulled her to him in a rough embrace. She laid her head on his shoulder and wrapped her arms tightly around him.

"Beloved, you know your father will never allow you to marry me now. He doesn't believe in having more than one wife."

"Then he won't know it until it's too late." He covered her protests with his fingers. "I'll plant my seed in your belly, and then he'll not refuse to acknowledge you."

As he talked, he calmly unfastened the tie from her right shoulder. She put her hand up to stop him, but withdrew her hand and slowly nodded. He unwrapped the rough wool from around her. As his eyes feasted on her nakedness, her eyes gradually lost their fear and took on a fateful determination. He stripped the wool from his own body and spread the garments out to make a kind of nest. It was a dreadful place to consummate a marriage, but if it was good enough for the sheep…and they might not have another chance.

It wasn't Er's first time, though he wouldn't have his father know that. Judah would be angry if he knew Er had gone in to harlots. So, Father was going to bring him a wife. What a surprise. He must have forgiven him for the sheep that got caught in the gorge and was found dead.

Er shoved Ruah down onto the cloaks and fell on her. If he wasn't gentle, it wasn't his fault, he decided. The rocks hurt his legs, and the fire within him demanded a quick release.

What would his bride be like? Would she submit as easily as Ruah? Fresh tears were in Ruah's eyes. He had hurt her, but she hadn't made a sound. It was natural the first time, they said. She would soon learn. And so would his other wife. He would take turns. He felt his seed release inside of her, but he was confused. He didn't feel satisfied.

Ruah lifted her ugly hands to bring his face near enough to kiss. "Why don't we just tell your father that we are now already married, my husband? Then he won't make you marry that other woman at all."

He was alarmed at the possibility that Ruah might blurt out the truth the first time she saw his father. Calming himself, he withdrew to lie beside her and stroke her belly and thighs.

"Don't be such a fool, Ruah. Father would be so angry with us, he would sell you to be someone's slave, or even as a harlot. He would do it, you know. You're still a slave, and he'd believe you unchaste." Her lower lip was trembling. He had frightened her sufficiently. He mustn't overdo it though or she would never be able to pretend.

"It is better to do things my way, my Dove. Come now, don't fret. You're now my wife, and I'm still excited. I'll show you what I wish.

As she finally left, his final order was that she return to him every day until his father returned. He smiled at her quiet nod.

Ruah combed her tangled mass of hair. She yelped as she came to a clump of matted grass and dirt, or whatever it was. She closed her eyes as she combed. She had loved Er since they could both walk. He loved her too; he had to. Even if he hadn't always been nice to her. He was just so full of life, sometimes he forgot to think about other people. He liked beautiful things, and she wasn't all that beautiful, but at least Er must think that she was. He had wanted to come in to her for many months, but she had laughed off his attempts until today. He was right. It was the only way to convince his father. A man could use a woman without a thought, but once she was carrying a babe of his flesh in her belly, it was as if she were Astarte in the flesh. However, becoming a wife was not quite as she had always dreamed it to be. It hurt.

As she picked out another knot, disillusioned tears streamed from her eyes. Every muscle ached, and her stomach was a little nauseous. Er had given her no pleasure at all, but she hadn't expected him to. It was said that some women enjoyed it, but sex was for men and having babies. A sweet little baby in her arms with Er's eyes and smile would give her pleasure. It would be worth the pain then. She would endure anything if Er loved her. She would give him all that he wanted. Anything, if only he wouldn't marry anyone else. Why did he even want that other woman?

It was fortunate that Mother was busy with the messenger so that Ruah could sneak into the tent unseen. For the first time in her life she was glad that a slave's garments were all the same brown wool, and that her mother wouldn't know that her tunic had been stained with the blood of her virginity. She would hide it in case the Master demanded it as proof that Er was her husband. Not that he would deny it. Yah grant that she would soon conceive so that Er could claim her as his wife before his wedding to the stranger.

A night of feasting and dancing due a true daughter of the house, such as Ashuah had always said would one day be Ruah's, was now the right of a stranger. Ruah had held Er off for so long so that she would be able to claim that right. Instead, she had been taken as what she truly was, a slave, in spite of their promises, perhaps also to be a slave-wife, a second to the unknown bride. If the woman was very beautiful and won Er's heart, she might be able to convince him to send Ruah away as Abraham's wife had done to Hagar, his Egyptian slave-wife. Even a child hadn't protected her. "Oh Hagar, tell me what I must do."

"Oh Yah, what must I do to escape my distress?" Tamar found it difficult to concentrate on her prayers. The men were standing near the fire saying their evening prayers also.

Rather too loudly, as usual. What had she done to offend Yah? How could she marry the Master's son when her fingers longed to feel the sweat-glazed skin of the father? Father had taught her that a woman must will to love her husband, but she had never willed to love the Master. He had appeared before her as one of Yah's angels. With the sun almost directly over his head, she had looked up at him from the ground, and it was as though she were looking into the face of Yah himself.

He was not Yah though. Yah could not be so cruel, or at least she had never thought He could. The Master had called her his wife, but one did not usually give a wife away, especially not to a son. Perhaps she should go to him again in the night. It might work. It almost had last time. But…

"Little One, are you still praying? You must come closer to the fire before you become chilled. The great God Yah can read your heart from over here."

Gently, the Master raised her and walked her over to the blazing campfire. As he sat down beside her and began telling stories of his ancestors, she was warm and unafraid despite the howling of the jackals and lions in the distance. His soothing voice became softer and softer as the bonds of sleep closed her eyelids. She dreamed her head lay in his lap while his arms held his cloak tightly around her. The mountain and the future it held for her were yet far away, but already she lay in their shadow and her gentle dream soon turned to nightmare. Something was heavy upon her. She could not breathe. She tried to scream but could not.

Chapter 5

"So this is my new daughter-in-law. Your messenger did not tell us she was so lovely. Welcome to my home, Tamar." Ashuah's embrace was warm and friendly, and Tamar was immediately stricken by guilt over her love for the husband of Ashuah.

"Thank you, Mistress. Your husband has told me much of your family on our journey. I am pleased to meet you at last."

The Master's brows slanted upwards slightly as though his wife's cordial greeting puzzled him. Though he had not said, he had hinted on their journey that the Mistress would not be pleased by Tamar's arrival. Ashuah had a great affection for Deborah, the wife of Oni, and she wished the marriage of their children. As he introduced Tamar to his sons Er and Onan, the Mistress called for the babe to be brought to her. Still wrapped in the tight bindings that would shape his head and limbs, the child hushed as his mother placed him into his father's arms to receive his blessing. Tamar stood back and watched with a detachment she didn't quite understand. Er, her husband-to-be, was not at all as she had expected. He was not much taller than she was, and had not even the beginnings of a beard. Nevertheless, his eyes were the eyes of a man, not a boy. He looked at her too long, too hard, as Ben Qara had done. She should run from those eyes, but she was just too tired. Her troubles must be making her imagine lust where there was none, only the foolishness of a boy.

The other son, Onan, never looked at her at all. He was about the same height as his brother, but thinner. He was much too pale for one who spent his days out in the sun. One bony hand rubbed across the edges of his teeth while the other twisted a little circle of his curly black hair.

The Master sat on a rock with the baby gripped between his knees, his eyes and hands lifted to heaven. While Judah's voice chanted blessings on the babe, his chubby little fists patted his father's legs as if demanding to receive a full measure of his father's blessings. Master Judah laughed and added several more blessings, and silently Tamar added her own small prayers for a fruitful life full of Yah's grace.

Oni had gone aside on their arrival to greet the two women Tamar guessed to be his wife and daughter. She wondered if the women hated her for coming here. She wouldn't blame them if they did. She would probably feel the same way in their place. Besides, she didn't like the idea of her marriage to Er any more than they did. She watched Ashuah rubbing her husband's shoulders while he lifted his son high up in the air and jiggled him lightly. He was an excellent father, it seemed. If only he weren't also a matchmaker.

"We have constructed a new tent at the end of the path for our young guest, my husband," Ashuah informed him proudly. "I thought perhaps Ruah might serve her there until her marriage." They exchanged a glance, but the Master did not question his wife's decision. He handed her the baby.

"You have worked quickly, Wife. I am sure that Tamar will appreciate your efficiency. She has brought with her some magnificent blankets and fabrics. Her mother is a master weaver, and has taught her this artistry. You should find a few of the cleverer servant girls to be taught by her there when the heat of the sun demands quiet activity."

"I will send Sheba and Kisse to her. They are both bright girls and will learn quickly." She turned to Tamar with new respect. A weaver was a glad addition to any household. "My own fingers are not at all clever with fine needlework, although I am a good tentmaker and my husband need never complain of wet feet even in the worst of the winter rains." She waited for Judah's nod before she continued. "I hope you will soon feel at home in our family."

Again, guilt ate at Tamar. Master Judah looked a bit worried. However, Ashuah seemed sincere.

"Thank you, Mistress. I am certain that I will." She was not certain. Far from it. Especially when she looked at Er. He was like a lion that had not eaten for many weeks, with his eye on a tender lamb. Moreover, Ruah paced in the distance like the lion's mate.

"Now, let us see all the good things you have brought us from the evil city." The Mistress started toward the caravan. "I cannot wait to see what that is!" As she pointed to the ox-cart carrying the giant oven, the Master laughed.

"That is a gift from our friend Hirah to the young couple. He says they can make cakes in it without ashes."

The Mistress climbed aboard the wagon and examined the oven with all the delight Tamar had displayed.

"I will be sending the oxen back to Hirah in a few days with instructions for something else I wish to buy. If you desire it, I will have him buy you another oven like this one."

The idea plainly interested her. "Let us see how well this one works first. Then we will consider it. Do you cook well also, my child?"

"No, Mistress. Not very well. Mother was attempting to teach me, but I have not a great deal of talent for it." She bowed her head.

"It is no matter. I will teach you. Would you mind if we put your wonderful gift down by my tent until your marriage? In the heat of the day, you can teach my girls weaving, and in the evenings, I will teach you to cook. Together we can try out the new cooking device." Ashuah dismounted the wagon and began to inspect the rest of the caravan's more usual wares.

"I would be delighted to do as you suggest, Mistress." Tamar tagged along beside her.

"How soon shall we hold the wedding?" As she spoke, the Mistress gave her a little hug, but her question was directed at Judah.

"I thought we might give them a little while to get to know each other. Er's birthday is in two months time. How would you like to hold the feast then?" He did not wait for her answer before he continued. "They are already officially betrothed, and the bride price has been paid, but her father wished her to remain with us until the marriage. I had wished for Er to return to Chezib with a kid for a widow and some gifts for the bride's family, but I will send servants with those. Er will have plenty of time to meet Tamar's family after the wedding."

"Lovely. He could not wish for a more beautiful birthday, could you, my child?"

Er had come up behind them without Tamar realizing it. "No, Mother. I could only wish that my birthday were tomorrow." Almost everyone laughed.

The Master declared that homecoming was a good reason to have a feast. He slaughtered a ram and roasted it himself over the large open fire. The Mistress busily organized the young servants to peel and cut onions, shell and chop nuts, and slice melons and figs. Tamar had never in her life seen so much food being prepared for one meal. Emi would live many weeks on half of what was served. The Mistress would let her do nothing. She was to rest. For this night, she was a princess with nothing more to do than to radiate her loveliness. Her mother would laugh at such an extravagant comment.

Whatever she might say about her lack of cleverness at weaving, the Mistress's hands were the best at cooking Tamar had ever known. Besides the lamb, they had locusts and frogs roasted until they were light and crunchy, leeks and onions in a garlic broth, raisin cakes topped with honey-coated almonds, cucumbers, olives, figs, dates, and melon soaked in wine. The firelight was enticing, and the Mistress kept pressing more food upon her. It seemed the first time in her entire life that she had felt so completely full after a meal. She should not eat so much, but she did not like to refuse on her first day, and besides, it was so lovely to indulge for just one evening. She would have to be careful in the future if so much food was generally served though. Father said that overeating was a sin against Yah.

Even though Er was not obvious, his gaze burned into her skin while she ate. To be fair, she also had watched the men as they ate their feast. Er had devoured his food, as she had known he would, and Onan played with his like a toddler instead of a nearly grown man. But their father—he had leaned back and savored every bite in a manner that had made her hungry belly groan. Er was handsome; there was no doubting that. His dark eyes and ruddy complexion in the firelight seemed to glow with youth and vitality while his father's seemed so tired.

"Is he not the most wonderful man Yah has ever created?" Ruah asked from behind her.

"Yes, he is." Tamar was referring to Judah, but Ruah clearly meant Er. She looked carefully at the servant who made no effort to disguise her love for the young man Tamar was soon to marry. Tamar felt sorry for her, though Ruah would probably despise her pity.

Trying to make conversation with the girl was difficult. "Has your family always lived in this place?"

Ruah cocked her head as if to ask if she were joking or merely stupid. "No, of course not. We follow the pasturelands and the water. Even though the Master has many vineyards and wheat fields, his first love is still for his sheep. Stewards remain behind to care for his farmland while we are gone, but only the Master is in charge of his sheep." She wiped her hands on her tunic. "Even when he has Er and Onan to take care of the herds while he goes on business, he questions them endlessly concerning their care and never seems satisfied. Er is a good shepherd, even if he does get a bit irritated at the stupid sheep sometimes." Ruah's lower lip protruded and her jaw became set.

Why must Ruah defend Er against an unmade attack? Tamar was biting her right thumb while she listened to the girl ramble on. She was already picking up the Master's habits. She must watch herself. Moreover, she must watch Ruah.

In the long conversations during their travel homeward, Tamar had learned that Ruah, and indeed her father and mother, were house-born slaves to the house of Jacob. Oni's father had come from the land of the Chaldeans with Abraham and Sarah as Abraham's most trusted servant. When she asked why his father had given him such a valuable slave if he were not a favored son as he claimed, Judah had surprised her by answering in the gruff tone he had used on Ben Qara that his father was an exceedingly foolish man when he grew jealous.

As she noted Oni's reddened face, she hastened to hide her curiosity, but Oni had spoken up. "When the Master's father had his youngest son born to him, his wife Rachel knew that she was dying, and never giving my name a thought, she named her son BenOni, the son of her sorrow. The Master's father grew furious, and he beat me near to my death. I could not convince him that I had never gone near to his wife. After he threw me out into the wilderness to die, the Master heard of my plight, found me, and dressed my wounds. He paid my full price to his father though I was already too old to be worth it."

The Master sat drawing little circles in the sand with a stick as though his compassion for the servant were a little thing made too much of by the grateful slave.

"Then he hid me," Oni continued, "until his father's wrath had cooled somewhat and I could return for Deborah and Ruah. Master Judah bought them for me too. Master Jacob changed his son's name to Benjamin, son of the right hand, but though the child is the image of his father, Master Jacob has never trusted me since, and he cannot bear my presence gladly."

Judah tossed down his stick and clasped the shoulder of the servant who seemed to be much more like a best friend. "As I said, my father is a fool when he is jealous. Let us talk of it no more."

Tamar had happily agreed. She felt a bond to the servant who had the same *go'el* she did. The Master trusted his servant completely, and now so did she. However, of his daughter, she was not so certain. Ruah's rambling speech revealed that the girl did not bear nearly the love for the Master that she did for his son. Tamar must keep her own counsel near Ruah lest the girl discover her true feelings and make life uncomfortable for everyone.

Alone in their tent, Tamar again tried to find out what life was like in the camp. Always the answers came back to Er, how good he was, how strong, how intelligent. Perhaps because she was to marry him, this was what Ruah thought she wished to hear. Her eyes lowered too often as if she were fearful she might actually have the effect she was supposedly trying to give.

Tamar lay back on the black wool cushion and watched as Ruah opened the bundles of fabrics and blankets Tamar had brought. As she lifted her mother's creations, Ruah was silent only a short time. Then she began to nod her head as she lifted each piece.

"Er will love this one. The colors are as rich jewels. This one will make him a fine cloak. He has always wished for the long sleeves of a man of leisure, but the Master says that all of his sons must work. Not that Onan works nearly as hard as Er does. It seems that every time he climbs the mountain, he falls down and injures himself severely and must rest several weeks to recover."

The cushion was soft, and as Tamar lay, not really listening anymore to the endless chatter, she almost fell asleep. She was in the midst of the dream where the sirocco wind blew again, and the Master fell down upon her to hide her in the cleft of the rock from the yellow dust that poisoned the air and withered the sparse grass and the wildflowers she had picked to make new garlands. He had kissed her then. He had not been able to help himself. Yah forgive her, she had wished many times since that the sirocco wind would blow again.

"I asked was your journey from Chezib very hard for you?" As Tamar's eyelids forced themselves open, Ruah's hands on her hips warned Tamar of her impatience. She seemed bold for a slave, but then Tamar had not had much experience with slaves.

"What?" Tamar sat up with her head in her hands and blinked. "No, not very. It was steep and rocky, of course, and the sirocco wind blew once so that we had to seek shelter from its might, but it was soon over."

Ruah gawked at her. "The sirocco wind, are you sure? It is weeks too late in the year for the sirocco."

Tamar shrugged. *Tell that to the wind.* Perhaps Yah had made it especially to show the Master his true feelings for her and call off this marriage. If so, it hadn't worked. She was still to be the bride to the wrong man unless Yah could do better than a wind of poison air.

Chapter 6

"We did it, Er! We did it!" Ruah waded through the sheep in her usual fashion, bouncing even more in her excitement, but she barely caught his attention this time. Ruah had come to him many times and although she was always willing, images of the smaller paler-skinned bride had taken her place in his thoughts. Once he had taken Tamar also, maybe her image would fade and give him peace, but for now, his blood surged within him. Oh well, Ruah would ease him for a time, but if only she would not lie so docile to his demands. Had she no spirit? The new one would not give in to him so readily. What in the name of Yah was Ruah yelling about?

"Did what?" He snatched the bag of food she carried from her hands and dove into it without waiting for her answer.

"Can't you guess?" She pried his fist from the bag and teased the fig he held into his mouth. When he made no reply but reached for another, she took his hand and patted it to her belly.

A piece of the fig caught in his throat, and tears came to his eyes as he choked. "You are lying. I don't believe it."

"Why would I lie about it?" she asked, rubbing his back until he breathed normally again. "Come on, Beloved. Let us go tell your family. This is what we've been waiting for, isn't it? Now your father will call off your other marriage." She pulled on his arm to go with her down the mountain.

"Now I understand. You can't possibly know for sure yet. It's too early. However, my wedding is in two days time, and you're jealous because she is so much more beautiful than you are. You're saying this to keep me from having her." He shoved her away from him. "But it won't work. I don't believe you."

"That is not true, my Beloved." Her voice was irritating with a whining tone. "I am with child. You will see. Everyone will soon see." She buried her face in her calloused red hands.

"As long as they don't see before my marriage feast," he warned. "I tell you now, my wife, I will have you both or I will have neither. If you speak one word of this, I will claim that the child you are carrying is not mine; that you have played the harlot to every hireling in the camp." He slapped her so hard she fell back onto the rocky ground. "Do you understand me?" he asked, drawing his hand back to strike her again.

She nodded, and he lowered his hand.

"I am not the wife who is the whore. Your father's castoff will not be so beautiful to you either after you have planted a baby in her belly. That is, at least, if your father hasn't already done so." She hid the sneer on her face as his hand came down again, but he didn't strike her this time, only jerked her back to her feet.

"What are you talking about, woman? Tamar is no harlot. She is the daughter of the Man of God, and Father bought her from him for me." His hand squeezed her face.

"After he found her naked in the street and bought her back from her rightful husband. Her family was gone from the town, but your father stayed in her home with her throughout the night. How many times do you think he could have come in to her before my father arrived with the dawn?" As he released her and backed away, her smile was triumphant.

"Where did you hear such nonsense?" he asked slowly.

She shrugged. "Mostly from our fathers, when they didn't know I was near. I heard bits and pieces and was finally able to put the story together. However, the messenger who took the gifts to Chezib confirmed it. It seems the town is full of stories of the godlike Hebrew who rescued the young maiden and carried her off to his palace in Hebron to be his bride."

"You're lying to me again!" Er slashed his staff across her left shoulder to her right breast, tearing the coarse wool and leaving an angry welt.

Even as she crumpled at his feet, Ruah defied him. "I guess you'll know on your wedding night, husband, when your seed mingles with that of your father. So what if you have not the blood of her virginity, you can have a big bellied wife to bear a child you can never be certain is yours." She began to laugh as though she would never stop.

Er began to beat her with his fists, and then gripped the already torn wool and ripped it its entire length until she lay completely naked in the sun. "Is this how she looked when my father found her?"

She nodded, still giggling in her hysteria.

"And yet her husband was not man enough to take her? How could that be?" His breathing was rapid and shallow, his face reddening beneath the heat of the sun though it could not begin to pierce the cold inside his heart.

Ruah sought to pull the pieces of cloth back together, but he slapped her hand away. Tossing the shreds aside, he grasped her wrists and held them. "But this husband will be. I shall take her again and again, but I shall not mingle my seed with my Father's. If she bears a child, I shall have proof of my father's wickedness and I shall let her watch him die before I kill her also. Until then, I will come in to her often, because if you speak truth, it will be as gall to my father's throat every time I use her."

Ruah turned her face away.

"Why aren't you laughing, my dove? Isn't it your wish that I now hate that which before I loved? I shall plant my seed in her as the Canaanites do where it can never bear fruit. Like this!"

This time she didn't remain passive. She fought him, but her strength was puny against his. Her cries fed his ecstasy. There would be blood like this on his wedding blankets too. Tamar's blood. Why had Yah destroyed Sodom and Gomorrah? Did he not know, as they had learned, that there was pleasure in pain?

"Ruah, what has happened to you? Here, let me help you to lie down."

When Tamar had settled the girl onto her mat and propped her with goat hair cushions, she found the wine bag and poured a generous portion down Ruah's throat. The servant seemed dazed, staring ahead and moving stiffly.

"Who did this to you?" she asked, wiping the girl's face and arms with a piece of wool dipped in wine.

"Fell down the ravine," Ruah mumbled as she closed her eyes. Covering her with her own blankets, Tamar saw the red streak across Ruah's breast and all the blood on her torn garment. Memories of her own brutal beating by Ben Qara were too fresh for her to believe Ruah had simply fallen.

"I must go to get your mother and the Master. Don't worry. I will return quickly."

"No, please." Ruah jerked upright. "He mustn't know. He will beat me and send me away."

Tamar returned to her and sat. "The Master is a good man; you do not need to fear. He would never send you away for what someone else has done to you." *Would he?*

Ruah sniffled. "Yes, yes, he would. He would deny it, and then I would be sent away as a harlot. He told me so."

"Who told you so?" Tamar wished to help the girl, but the Master would demand to know the name of the assailant. Tamar shook her by the shoulders. "Who did this to you, Ruah?"

As she turned away, Ruah muttered, "No one. I told you I fell down the ravine."

She had to get someone. The girl needed help, but she did not want it from Tamar. If not the Master, then whom should she get? Maybe the Mistress could make her see it was best to tell before someone else was hurt. Tamar found the Mistress with Deborah, bending over the large oven in front of her tent. When Tamar explained what was wrong, both women left their work and ran to Tamar's tent. She ran back and forth several times to deliver water, ointment and scraps of cloth for bandages, and then paced outside while the women talked to Ruah. The Mistress finally lifted the tent flap.

"Did she tell you what had happened?" Tamar was shaking with anxiety.

"Only that she had fallen down the ravine." Ashuah took Tamar by the shoulder and lead her down the hill toward her own tent.

The camp was large; most of the tents were much larger than any of the houses in Chezib. As they had approached the encampment, from the distance she had indeed thought it was a town. The flat roofs of black goat hair gleamed in the sunlight. When she had entered her own tent, she had been amazed that only two people lived in such a space. The Master and Mistress's tent was even larger. The nine poles stretched as far apart as they could without sagging.

As they stepped into the tent and moved to the Mistress's side, it was like entering the inner recesses of a bear's cave. With black mats lining the floor and clay lamps glowing in the corners even in the daytime, she shivered despite the intense summer heat.

"Tell me what Ruah told you, child." Ashuah spoke quietly and handed Tamar the wineskin, coaxing her to take a good swallow.

"Only that the Master would sell her as a harlot if she tells."

Ashuah nodded slowly and murmured to herself. "Then she has not only been beaten, but someone has come in to her as well. I thought as much. I felt her belly as I washed her wounds, and it was tight like that of a woman with child."

"Did you ask her of this, and yet she still would not tell?"

The Mistress shook her head. "I said nothing of my suspicions. Deborah is my friend, and it would hurt her to know that her daughter has deceived her. I may yet be wrong."

Fear washed through Tamar. Ruah would only lie to protect one person; the person Tamar was to marry in two days time. It was more important than ever that she tell the Master so he would call off the wedding.

Ashuah brightened her voice, "Fortunately, for Ruah's sake, my husband has gone off to oversee the barley harvest. He will only return just in time for the marriage feast." She put her arms around Tamar. "Come; let us not spoil such a happy occasion for you with such evil thoughts. If Ruah has a husband, she will tell us when she is ready."

It could not be soon enough.

Chapter 7

On the day of her wedding, Tamar's spirit was alone like a sheep utterly lost in the desert. Why had her father given up all thought of traveling to Hebron after he returned to Chezib and consented to this marriage? It was as though his mission were accomplished. She had dreamed that he told her not to be frightened. However, her hands still trembled. If Yah cared so much for His people, as her father said He did, why did He allow this? Why did Father allow it?

All through the morning while the Mistress and Deborah had fussed over her, bathing her, and rubbing her with myrrh-scented unguents, Ruah had thrown looks filled with such hollow-eyed hatred that Tamar was more certain than ever that Er was the husband who had beaten her and fathered the child she would not yet admit she carried.

The floor-length linen tunic the Mistress wrapped around her was the softest fabric she had ever worn. Though it was the finest embroidery work her mother had ever made, it was as sackcloth to her. The loops of gold around her wrists and hanging from her ears were the wheels of a funeral cart that would bear her body to its grave. The Mistress and Deborah had wished to pierce her cheeks with rows of rubies and emeralds as they had heard was now the custom of some brides, but this she refused, allowing them only to place two small rubies in her nose. Tamar had painted her own face, preferring the gentle powders her mother made to the garish coloring of the Canaanites to which the Mistress was accustomed. How could people who seemed to love color as much as they did live in black tents with no end to the monotone?

The marriage feast was to be even more elaborate than the homecoming celebration on the night of her arrival. Oni had overseen the slaughter and dressing of his Master's best fatted-calf. Throughout the day, it had filled the camp with its aroma, a smell fragrant even to the nose of Yah. To her it was a loathsome odor reminding her of her imminent marriage.

The Master returned with the breeze before the setting sun. If only she could run to him, to hide in his cloak crying out that his son was an evil man, more evil even than Ben Qara. But she dared not. He would not believe her; only think that she was cold and unwilling to marry any man at all.

The music of the feast began. Servants played timbrels and beat drums, plucked lyres and sang songs they made up as they danced to the exuberant rhythms. They praised Yah for the beauteous young Tamar, and the prowess of the shepherd, Er, and the children a fruitful union would bring forth. Inside her tent, she covered her ears to block out the blessings poured upon her.

It was customary for the groom to come to the house of the bride on the wedding day and take her from there to the home of his father for the marriage feast. She had been carried away from her home over two months ago, and not by the groom, but by his father. The feast would go on for days, but before the coming dawn, Er would bring her back to this tent and make her his wife. Would it not be wonderful if she could dress Ruah in her place as Laban had done with Leah to the Master's father Jacob? But Ruah was not near enough to her size, and Er would never be fooled.

She pulled the veil down over her grim face and fastened it with a golden band, then sat to wait for her husband.

When Er finally appeared, his festal apparel made her bridal finery seem simple. A long-sleeved white tunic reached to his ankles. Over this, two large diamonds fastened a scarlet apron vest at his shoulders. Sapphires and emeralds embellished the embroidered edging of the vest and across the bands of the many layers of his turban. His cassia perfume "came before him strongly" as the Master would say, but not as though he were filthy from days in the field, only vain. So many gold bits hung from his neck and arms she wondered that he could walk. The Master must indeed be a Prince that he could so array his son, even for a marriage feast. As she reached to blow out the tent lamp, Er stayed her hand.

"No, my little bride. There will be no darkness in the tent when I take you. I wish to see what my father has purchased for me."

The angry tone made her tremble but he turned without another word. As they came out of her tent, she saw that the camp was everywhere lit with torches and campfires. It was as though the entire city of Hebron had assembled on the hillside to join in the celebration. The cadence of the drums pounded into her head like a tent nail but Er strutted in front of her like one about to ascend to the throne of Yah.

The tents in the camp formed a large circle. The distance between her tent and the Master's was only a small part of that circle, but this night it was as a journey of many days, which yet ended far too soon.

Her eyes sought out the Master. He was in the midst of his family, falling on his brothers' and father's and grandfather's necks, weeping openly in his joy that they had come. The young man with the reddish beard had to be Ben-Oni. He was the image of a young Jacob, only with kinder, gentler eyes, like the eyes of the Master when he laughed, like the eyes of his Grandfather Isaac.

She had heard much to make her hate the Master's father, yet he was so befitting of the picture she had made of him in her mind that she could not. She could only feel sorry for the man who had claim to such love from so many and yet wanted no part of it. He limped slightly, and many of the younger ones offered to help him find a place to sit on the rocky hillside, but he would not suffer to be touched by any of his grandsons, not even Er on his wedding day. At this rebuff, the first pang of sympathy for her husband tugged her heart. Er betrayed no outward sign of the rejection and was soon dancing wildly with his uncles and male cousins.

Tamar went to sit with her mother-in-law and her women guests. They plied her with many dishes she had never seen before, including a dish of boiled mandrakes that they said would make her relax for her night's work, and which Ashuah whispered to her would help her to be soon with child. Without protest, she ate the mandrakes and sampled the other dishes set before her though she could not have told anyone what she had eaten even moments later. Ashuah kissed her cheek and left her alone while she and her guests went to make sure all the servants were fed.

Er drank much wine as the men offered up their blessings upon him. The evening was not yet far advanced, and yet he was already walking with a crooked gait. The Master also drank much, but he had told her it took much to make him drunken, and it seemed it was true. If Er fell asleep, perhaps he would not come to her. She sat in her place all alone while the men danced about on the hillside. A hand tapped on her shoulder.

"Well, Little One, are you ready to become a wife?" She looked up to see the Master standing beside her, and breathed a sigh of relief that Er was still dancing to the wild rhythm.

She shook her head. "No, Master, but I will do as you have commanded. Such love I bear for you."

He looked around, but no one had heard. "You must not say such a thing ever again, child. You are my daughter-in-law, not my wife."

"I promise, Master. I am glad that your family came tonight. At least it gave you a time to fall on your father's neck. He is a hard man, but he will forgive you when your brother returns."

Judah backed away from her, his face red. "Is this a threat to make me marry you instead of my son? If so, I'll…."

"No, of course not, Master." She jumped to her feet, tripping on the hem of the long tunic. As he caught her, she sobbed into his broad chest, "I'm sorry, Master. I did not mean to make you angry."

"I think it is time that I claimed my bride." Er glared at her, his handsome face ugly. Tamar realized that the music had stopped, as well as the dancing, and many of the guests were staring at them. She backed away from the Master and turned to her husband. A flute began playing a strange melody that echoed through the camp. Everyone turned to try to find the flute player, but he was not visible. As she followed Er back up the path to their tent, Tamar saw Onan high up in an oak tree, sending notes through the air with the fervency of a prophet sending a message to the deaf ears of Baal.

Chapter 8

"How did you meet my father?" Er confronted her as soon as she had lowered the tent flap behind her.

"What?" She stepped back against the tent flap.

He grabbed her arm and pulled her further into the tent. "You won't be able to run to my father this time, wife. I asked you how you met my father, and I demand an answer!"

"He...he came to Chezib to see my father."

"Liar!" He ripped the veil from her face. "Now, take off your clothing, Lovely Tamar, that your husband may see what has already been seen by an entire town of leering men."

"How did you know?" She moved toward the entrance, but he blocked her path.

"Never mind that. Do as I said."

Slowly she unfastened the silver pin that held her garment at the shoulder, and dropped the tunic to the floor. The unguents her mother-in-law had rubbed on her body made it shine in the light of the clay lamp hanging behind her. At his bidding, she removed the bracelets from her wrists and ears as well as the tiny rubies from her nose. All she had left on were the soft leather boots.

"Remove them, too." His voice was rough.

As she complied, she decided that she had best be as calm as possible if she would not make him angrier.

"Can we not talk of this later, my husband? Surely you would prefer to enjoy our new relationship." She chewed on her thumb.

He moved closer, lifting her long black tresses to gain a better view. "Yes, it would be lovely to come in to you, would it not?"

Shaking, but trying to hide her fear, she lay back on the cushion and held out her hand to him. "I am yours to take when you will, husband."

"No, not yet, you little fox." He turned away from her. "You are too anxious; too anxious by far for an innocent virgin. Ruah was right. My father has planted his seed in you, and now you wish me to claim his child."

She jumped to her feet. "What? No! Er, you are wrong! Your father is a good man. He would never do such a thing!" She placed her tiny hands flat against his gold-laden chest. "I was anxious that you not learn the truth. It's true when your father rescued me, I was naked in the street being beaten by a man who had claimed to buy me for his son. He tried to lie with me right there in the street, but your father stopped him. No man has lain with me, my husband. My blood will prove that to you."

Sneering, Er thrust her hands from him. "How can I believe that when you allowed my father to stay the night with you alone in your own house? Blood is easily drawn by wily brides who wish to deceive love-blinded husbands, my lovely liar. It proves nothing."

"We were not alone." She shook her hair forward and covered her face with her hands. "An old woman from my town stayed with us through the night."

"And she didn't sleep at all, this old woman, but kept vigil of your honor all night long? What kind of a fool do you take me for?" He jerked her hands from her face, but she could not meet his eyes as much because of the fear of his fury as for the knowledge that Emi had had just the opposite idea of how to save her honor.

"No. I will not lie to you, my husband. She slept. But your father did not come in to me, I tell you." She shook her head wildly. "He would have kept me for himself if he had. Then he would never have given me to you."

Er thrust her back onto the cushions. "And you would have liked that, wouldn't you? Now I see. You wanted a rich man, not his shepherd son. Perhaps he didn't uncover you in the night. Perhaps it was you who came to him." Her sharp intake of breath gave away that he had come upon the truth. "So it was like that. He didn't want you, but he couldn't resist."

"You are wrong! He did resist. We talked through the night. He did not come in to me." She laid her head on her elbow. "You do not understand. I was disgraced in the eyes of my people, and I had to have a husband."

"Talked? Talked of what? You know nothing of the life of a shepherd, and my father hates cities so much that he lets Hirah handle most of his business so he can avoid going into them." His question was the first sign that he might be beginning to believe her.

"I cannot tell you that. You must trust me."

The ugly sneer returned. "Trust you? I must trust you, you say, when you have admitted that you attempted to trick my father into marrying you?" He put his hand to his chin as if he were considering. "I will give you this choice. For three months, you will allow me to come in to you as the Canaanites do. Then, if your belly is not big with my father's child, we will talk again of trust." He fell down beside her and pushed her hair aside, sliding his hands over her skin.

"No, Er, you must not! Yah forbids it. Such is the manner of men!"

"And of hierodules. You will be my own temple whore. Perhaps I shall even make you wear a veil so that no man but me will ever again look upon that temptress face." Writhing, she managed to escape, but he caught her hair, and wound it in his strong grasp.

"You cannot do this evil to me!" She beat him with her tiny fists.

"I can, and I will. If you do not submit to me gladly, I will beat you, and it would be a sin to mar these luscious breasts."

She gasped. "It was you who beat Ruah!"

He shrugged. "I was just practicing. You would not want me to tear you for want of knowledge, would you?"

How was it possible that Yah could make such an evil man to be the son of one so noble? "Were you also practicing when you planted your child in her?"

"She told you that?" He gripped her hair even tighter, and pulled her beside him. "I will kill her for betraying me. Do you understand me?"

She could not cease quivering, but was determined not to give voice to her fear. "Ruah did not betray you. She loves you so much that she foolishly kept silent even after you had beaten her. But she didn't have to tell that she was with child. When your mother tended her wounds, she felt how hard her belly was."

His attention was diverted from her for a time. "Ruah told me the truth then. And mother knows. Why did she not stop our marriage then, I wonder?"

"I don't know."

"No, no wait. I do. It makes sense. If you are married to me, you cannot take away her husband. I do my mother a service by making you my hierodule. Oh, and also, you will be slave to Ruah, my first wife. Now, come to me!"

"No!" She tried again to get away. "You had best go ahead and kill me now. I don't love you, Er, and I will gladly tell everyone how evil you are."

"Ah, but you will not, my wife. You have told me who you do love, and I will kill him also." His evil laughter filled the tent.

Judah sat alone at the spot where Tamar and Er had left him. As he surveyed the crowd that had assembled on the mountainside to celebrate with him, he wondered that he should be so distressed over the loss of the Little One. Like his father, he had always had the ability to bring wealth to his family. Yah had blessed him with three strong sons. Were these not all the blessings a man needed? Why was one child-woman so important to him?

"Master, you must stop her." Judah flinched when Ruah fell at his feet sobbing. "You cannot let her have him. He is my husband, not hers."

"Stop this nonsense, Ruah. I know you and Er had planned to marry, but that has changed. Er is Tamar's husband now." He lifted her to her knees. "We have many guests and they need to be served." Her bruises caught his attention. "What has happened to you, child? Who has beaten you?"

Ruah waved away his questions. "You do not understand, Master. Er took me as his wife over two months ago. I bear his child. Oh, please don't send me away. I am not a harlot. I loved him so much that I let him take me so that you would not part us. I would lose him to her if I did not."

As she began to weep, he gathered her into his arms for a time to stay her fears. "Of course I will not send you away, child. You are my daughter now. Why did you not tell me of this before now?"

Tokens of Promise

Ruah trembled. "Er would not have you to know, Master. He wished to have her also. And he is very angry with me."

Angry enough to beat his pregnant wife? Yah preserve his people. Judah tried to use a gentle voice. "Why was he angry, Ruah?"

Backing away from him, she knelt before him with her head in her hands. "Because I tried to stop him from marrying her. Master, I have done an evil thing. I told Er that you had come in to her while you were in Chezib, and perhaps she bore your child."

Although Judah had never before beaten her, Ruah cowered as though she expected a rod to strike her down. And he was angry enough to do so, had she already not made such a pitiful sight, and been so hurt by his own son. He spoke softly.

"You must think me a very evil man, Ruah, to believe that I would do such a thing to my own child. Why would you tell such a lie to Er? You claim to love him."

"I do, Master, but she is so beautiful that already she was winning his heart. Soon I would be like Hagar, sent out into the desert with my child."

"Well, it is too late. He has taken her by now. He has two wives in spite of his father's objections, and it seems he will reap the same strife my father did of it." He glanced over at his father standing alone under an olive tree gazing at the festivities but not participating in them.

"No, Master, you must stop him. Not for my sake or my child's, but for hers. He will hurt her, Master. He will make her pay for what he thinks you have done to her."

"What do you mean, hurt her?" He jumped to his feet and ripped off his long festal jacket.

"He did more than beat me, Master. He took me in the Canaanite fashion, and he promised..."

Judah took off running up the steep hill. *Yah curse the day the boy was born!* He was yet too far from the tent when he heard Tamar's screams.

When Judah opened the tent flap, Er turned a hideous grin at him. "You are too late, Father. You did not save her this time from her evil husband."

Er stood before his father naked and unashamed. Tamar crouched in the corner crying and hiding her face. She had wrapped herself in a blanket. Er followed his father's gaze to her blood on him. "Why did you enter my tent on my wedding night, Father? Did you wish a turn at my hierodule? Perhaps another time I will share her with you. I think she has had enough for now."

All the wrath of Yah filled Judah as he struck his son. "How dare you do this? You are no more a son of mine!"

Er laughed. "Thank you, Father. It is unlawful to strike one's father, and I wouldn't want to break your precious law."

Even as he issued this warning, his right hand landed a severe blow to his father's cheek. While Judah stooped over, stunned, Er armed himself with the heavy necklace of gold nuggets. Swinging it at his father's face like a sling, he managed to get behind Judah to try to strangle him with it. Holding the garrote away from his neck with one hand, Judah threw Er away from him. When Er hit the tent curtain wall, he must have grabbed the rope of the lamp, for it flew from its post and crashed down upon his head.

Judah knelt to the side of his son to feel the breath of the living. There was none. He was dead.

The flames from the lamp began to spread. Judah picked up the huddled Tamar and carried her from the burning tent.

Chapter 9

Judah laid the Little One down on the ground away from the tent and attempted to re-enter the smoldering structure. A crowd was hastening up the hill. Thank Yah goat hair did not easily burn. However, it had been a long dry season, and fire could spread quickly through the dried grass. Already there was more smoke than flames, and there would be time to put this out before it caused more damage.

Preparing to lift the body of his son, he stopped to wipe the smoke from his eyes and spied the Little One's boots. With Er over his shoulder, he snatched up the soft leather shoes and escaped.

"Back away, my friends," he called as he came out into the stinking air. "My son is dead."

As the people obediently began to back away, Ruah screamed and fainted. Oni and Deborah lifted her and carried her away to their tent. Judah bent to lay down Er's body, and dropped the shoes beside Tamar. Her eyes were wide open, staring at nothing, and she quivered as a lamb does when caught in the briars for a day and is near unto death.

As he called for a servant to come for Tamar and take her to the next tent, Ashuah came running up the hill tearing her long garment. She fell down on her dead son, weeping and moaning. Silently, Judah also tore his festal tunic down the middle and reached down to smear his forehead and cheeks with the ash-blackened dirt. His brothers and cousins did the same, and Reuben came forward to slash the long tent ropes with his knife so that the collapsed skins might smother what was left of the fire.

"Tell us what happened, Judah," one of the guests shouted.

"Yes, why did you run up the hill so fast and go into the bridal tent?" Another demanded. "I did not see any fire then."

Questions from all over the crowd rumbled without time for answers.

"Why was that lamp lit at all?"

"What is going on here?"

"How did you know?"

Judah held up his hands. "Please my friends, go home and leave us to bury our dead." He looked down at his distraught wife. "It was a horrible accident," he said firmly. "A simple case of an overly excited bridegroom knocking down the clay lamp onto his own head."

The questions persisted. "But why was the lamp lit? It is forbidden."

Judah stared at the grim face of his father. "Perhaps he had heard too many times the sad tale of how his grandfather Jacob was deceived in the darkness."

A few persevered, "Then why did you enter the tent?"

Judah shrugged. "I heard a scream."

Again, he lifted his arms and motioned them away. "I have answered your questions as much as you need to know. I thank you for coming, but as the occasion has turned from joy to sadness, my family needs time to mourn. Please, if you live too far away to return home tonight, let my servants know, and they will prepare tents for you."

Grumbling, most of the guests moved down the hill to gather their belongings to leave.

As he turned to go also, Jacob said gruffly, "You will not bury this child of a Canaanite in the tombs of Abraham and Sarah or by the grave of my beloved Rachel."

Judah didn't bother to keep the anger out of his voice. "Thank you Father, but I had no intention of doing so. It has been many years since I have needed to ask anything of you."

When the gentle arms of his grandfather Isaac offered to comfort him, Judah waved him away also with a murmured request for him to go instead to Jacob. Reuben was already organizing two servants to fetch the cart and spices to wash and dress the boy with, and another servant to lift Ashuah and help her to the tent where Er's body would be prepared for the grave. Then Reuben carried the body over his left shoulder while he steadied Judah on the walk down the hill.

"Leave the women to prepare the body." Reuben laid Er on the mat. "Let us go dig out a suitable cave for the tomb." He led his brother Judah out of the tent.

"Thank you, my brother, but there is no need. There is a cave near the top of the mountain where my sons often played as children. If we can find stones large enough to lay him on and to cover the mouth of the cave, it should be a good place for him."

Reuben walked with him further down the path to Judah's tent. He lifted the flap. "Then sleep now, and when it is light, we will find your stones."

Judah lay down on his sleeping mat, and Reuben settled himself down on a camel saddle nearby. However, Judah was hardly down before he jumped back up.

"No, I cannot sleep now. First, I must check on the Little One and Ashuah…and Ruah fainted. She bears Er's child."

His words were becoming more and more incoherent, and Reuben move to catch Judah if he should faint. Finding the wineskin that hung from the center tent pole, he placed it to his brother's lips and demanded that he drink. After only a slight swallow, Judah seemed to revive somewhat. He pushed the wine away.

"No, I have already drunk too much this night for a clear head. I must see to the women."

"I will do that. Rest now. Your eyes declare that you have not slept well in a long while."

The commanding tone had its effect, and Judah lay down.

In the far corner of the next tent from the burnt bridal chamber, Reuben found Tamar lying curled up like a newborn babe. He crouched near her and used the gentlest voice he of which he was capable. "Are you the one my brother calls the Little One?"

Nodding, she struggled to find her own voice. "Is the Master all right?"

"No, he is worried about you and his wife. Shall I tell him you are better?"

Again she nodded, wrapping the blanket even tighter about her. "I have no clothing. Could you send someone to bring me a tunic? I must go to help the Mistress."

He had never been a fool, and the overly bloodied blanket gave hint of the truth of the night. Wed...Bed...Dead. Yah's vengeance could be swift to one who abused the elect. "Of course."

"You are Reuben, the Master's eldest brother, are you not?"

"Yes. How did you know that? Your father is a Man of God. Are you also a prophetess?"

She tilted her head as if the question had never before occurred to her. "I don't know. Only where the Master is concerned am I certain of some things. But he does not see my destiny as I do, so I must be wrong, and I cannot therefore be a prophetess, can I?"

She sat up and her dark eyes seemed to look at him like the eyes of Yah. "But I do know that the reason you did not subscribe to your brother's plot was that you felt already too heavy with your other sin against your father."

He gasped. "My brother told you..."

She shook her head. "No. Your brother does not even know the reason. Your father's concubine kept your secret well."

As his face reddened at her knowledge of his guilt, Tamar comforted him. "Please do not be angry and hate me for telling you this. Yah wishes only to comfort you. He has forgiven both you and your brothers for your actions, and He promises that out of all things, He has worked to make you all better men."

"And do you believe Yah can bring good out of the tragedy of this night?"

She sat back. "I must believe it, Master Reuben, or I could not continue to live the life Yah has appointed to me."

Oni bowed low as he entered the tent. "Master," he reported, "all has been taken care of. Your guests have all either left or been found a tent to sleep in for the rest of the night. Master Reuben has taken the watch until dawn. I tried to dissuade him, but he said he had much to think of, so I left him to do so in peace."

"What of the women?"

"All is prepared, and they are resting. Master Reuben and I both looked in on everyone."

Judah lifted himself up onto his elbows. "Then come in and sit, my friend. We have much to discuss. Do not bow before me. You are no longer my slave, but my family. It was agreed."

Oni sat cross-legged near enough to hear the weak voice. "Yes, Master," he affirmed, "it was agreed. But that was before. With things as they are, I cannot hold you to that agreement."

Judah turned onto one elbow to face Oni more directly. "Only because you are more honorable than I." Slowly he shook his head. "Why is that, my friend? I try so hard to do what is right, but so often it seems that what is right for one hurts another."

"I know, my son." Oni patted his shoulder. "If only we could have the wisdom of Yah, we should always know what is best for everyone."

Judah sat up and faced the problem. "Yes, well, since we don't, we must do what we can. And that means fairness to you. My son took your daughter; therefore, you and your family are free. If you will serve me, from now on it will be for wages. Or if you prefer, I will give you a bit of land for farming or a small herd of sheep."

Oni rubbed his eyes with his arm, tears glistening in his eyes. Freedom. What could it mean to one who had never known it, and how little to those who knew nothing else?

"Master, if it truly pleases you, I will continue to work for you. At my age I cannot begin a new life."

Judah took hold of Oni's right hand and placed it on his thigh. "I hope you will not change your mind as we discuss more unpleasant matters."

Shaking his head before he withdrew his hand, Oni reassured him, "No, my son, I feel I already know what it is you would say."

Judah lay back and stared up at the blackness. "I am not sure that you do, Oni. My son was quite filled with evil, and the shame of our children's relationship was mostly with him, though Ruah must bear a part of it, if small."

Oni nodded but remained silent.

"I cannot allow the child's cord to be tied. I am sorry, but conceived in evil, the child would be many times more evil even than his father."

"I understand, and I agree, Master. Yah would have us to put the evil from our tents."

"No! You cannot!" In the shadows, the pallid face of Ruah appeared as a specter.

Oni arose and went to her. "What are you doing here, daughter? You were to be in our tent resting."

She pulled away from him. "Don't call me daughter. You who call my husband evil would throw his innocent babe to the field to die even as it takes its first breaths of life. I am no longer your daughter, and I will leave now with my child as Hagar to the wilderness."

Judah's voice was harsh. "Do not be a fool, Ruah. Hagar was not pregnant when she left the camp, and yet she still almost died in the desert. Only her righteousness protected her, and you have no such claim. Where would you go? Your family is here, and unless they would go with you…"

Oni shook his head. "No, the Master is right. I forbid you to leave until the child is born. Then, if you wish, I am sure the Master can arrange a suitable marriage for you."

Ruah stared first at her father and then at Judah, blinking rapidly. "Is not my next marriage already arranged? I was Er's first wife. By law shall I not now be given to Onan?"

Judah shook his head vigorously and Oni turned his back to her.

Oni sighed. "Er never publicly claimed you as his wife, child. You have no rights at all. You were at best his concubine. The right to marry Onan belongs to Tamar."

"No, it cannot be!" Ruah flung herself at Judah, beating him with her fists.

Chapter 10

Ashuah shook her head and spoke softly. "She has lost the child, Husband. It is certain. The way of women has come upon her twice since our son's accident, yet she will not believe it. She will not even keep away from the men upon those days. No, she holds her belly and talks to a babe, telling it that she will run away at the last moment and thwart your evil plan to destroy it."

As they walked up the path together, Judah took his wife's arm to comfort her. His free hand scratched his chin where his beard was just filling out after shaving his face while mourning his son, but was not yet to the length he desired.

"Do you think me evil?"

"No, my lord, a bit harsh sometimes, perhaps, but never evil."

"Thank you for that, my love."

While they walked together silently, Tamar's words of the previous night before haunted him. She had said, "Master, may it be someday that you will love me as much as you love the wife you somehow believe you do not care for." Could it truly be that his father's hatred had blinded him so completely to his own feelings for Ashuah?

"Judah, what are you thinking? You would not harm Ruah for her sickness, would you?" She was tugging at his cloak to regain his attention.

"What? No...no, of course not, my love. She will surely be better with time. No, I was thinking of you. How well you have taken the death of your son, and all this foolishness with Ruah. I am so proud of you."

In the fading sunlight, he could see her cheeks redden like skin burned by the sun. How well she responded to a little praise, and how little he had given to her through the years. However, as he reached for her when they entered the darkness of their tent, she drew back from him slightly.

"There is something I must tell you first, my lord, and then you may not want to come in to me anymore. You may wish a new wife, and I release you to find one."

What evil could she have done, that she would think he might put her away? He hesitated. "What will you tell me, wife?"

She sighed. "Since Shelah was born, the way of women has ceased with me. It is doubtful that I will ever bear you any more sons or daughters." She hung her head.

Slowly he lifted her chin and kissed her. "I am not my father, Ashuah. I do not care that you will not have a child from it. From now on when I take you it will be for the sheer joy of it that we will both receive." It was joy; a sweeter joy than they had ever before known together.

"Good morning, Mistress." Tamar held out a brightly colored bundle to her.

"Good morning, child. What is this?"

"A present. Unfold it and see." She jumped up and down with the enthusiasm of Onan.

Ashuah left off chopping vegetables for the stew pot, and wiped her hands on her tunic. "Let me see, child. What is it?"

As she moved back to spread out the large blanket, Tamar held one edge so that it might not touch the ground. The blanket was the first large piece she had ever done without her mother's supervision, and she could hardly contain her hope that the gift might be pleasing to the Master and Mistress.

"If you look at it, and then close your eyes, you should see the mountain rocks and lupine grasses." Beneath the veil of mourning, Tamar's eyes closed to suit her words.

"Yah bless you, child. I don't need to close my eyes. This is the most beautiful piece I ever saw. These brightly colored bits are the wildflowers growing up between the mountain rocks, and the little gold specks are the beginnings of a sirocco wind that has already withered a few of the wildflowers. See here." She pointed to the smaller clusters at the top left.

Tamar covered her mouth with her hand. "I am so sorry, Mistress. Give the blanket back and I will destroy it immediately. I am horrified the picture is so vivid. I thought it was only in my mind." She lifted a silent prayer that Yah would forgive her.

"Hush, child, even Yah cannot be offended by your artistry. The picture is only in your mind, and in mine, and in all who have faced the mountain sirocco. I will cherish your gift." She folded the blanket and laid it on the mat beside the sleeping baby Shelah, and returned to her stew pot.

While Ashuah stirred the stew with a large flat stick, Tamar picked up the little double-edged chopping axe and quartered several onions. Her cooking lessons had gone well, and she felt much more comfortable with the axe. She sat down opposite the Mistress and lifted off the outer skins before dropping the pieces into the pot.

"You are so good, Mistress, and the Master is so good also…"

Ashuah laid down the stirring stick. "And you would know how it is that if I am good and the Master is good, we came to have such an evil son."

The slight tremble in her voice betrayed her fear of offending the Mistress. "Mistress, I did not mean to say…"

"No, of course you would not say it." She patted her arm. "You are yourself a good child…But I know the truth of my son's treachery to you. My husband told me the moment he felt I could bear the shock of it."

Sobbing, she dropped the little chopping axe and went to Ashuah's arms. "I'm sorry, Mistress. I did not mean that Er should die for what he did. I hated him at the time, but he was angry and...hurt himself when he...he..."

Pushing her hair back from her face, Ashuah rocked her as she often did Shelah. "You have nothing at all to be sorry for, Little One. Ruah's accusations were foolishness. She does not know my husband as I do."

Tamar drew back and gasped. "What?"

"Did you think I did not know?"

At Tamar's nod, Ashuah lifted Tamar's veil and wiped the tears that strayed down the girl's cheeks.

"How I wish I did not. Such evil is hard to bear in those you have loved their entire lives."

A cry from the baby diverted their attention. The Mistress picked up Shelah and placed him to her breast. "Let us talk of much more pleasant matters. Your days of mourning will be over in a month's time, and when you are given in marriage to Onan, you can be happy again. My son Onan is not at all like his brother. He will not hurt you, my child. I promise."

"I know, Mistress." She stood to take hold of the flat stick and gave the pottage a brisk stir then sat again to chop the rest of the vegetables into smaller than normal pieces with the axe.

The Mistress watched her. "Would you not love to one day have a babe at your breast like this one?"

Tamar looked out over the fields where Onan worked with his father. "Yes, Mistress. I would like that very much. I dream of such a day. Shelah is such a good babe, I hope..."

"You hope he grows to be as good a man. He will."

Tamar laughed. "And they call me a prophetess. Mistress, you are amazing. No wonder..."

"No, I am not amazing. I only believe that if we continue to strive for good, one day that good will come, if we wait upon Yah."

"But are you not a Canaanite, Mistress? How is it that…"

"That I believe in the God of my husband, and not the gods of my nation?"

Tamar nodded.

"I don't know. At first, perhaps it was just that I saw how much better Israelite men treated their wives than the men of Canaan. Especially my Judah. My mother tricked him into marrying me. However, he never held it against me. He has always treated me with all the respect of an Israelite wife. But as Judah told me the stories of his God; how Abraham came here from the land of Ur and all the promises Yah gave to him, how he took Abba Isaac up onto the mountaintop to sacrifice him but at the last moment Yah provided a ram in the thicket instead, how Jacob wrestled with an angel until he blessed him; all these stories became real to me because I knew them to be true. The gods of Canaan are wood and stone. What can they do? Yah is real. He is the only God who deserves my worship. This much I know."

Chapter 11

Ruah shaded her eyes as she looked up into the tree. "Come down here, Onan," she whispered.

"What do you want, Ruah?" His left hand continued fingering his flute though he had moved it from his mouth down against his chest. His right forefinger twisted the remains of a curl at the back of his head. He didn't look at her, as usual.

"Shhh...come down here so I can talk to you," she whispered louder.

"Shhh...No thank you, Ruah. I like it up here. Yup, you come up. Up-up-up, yup-yup-yup."

His resonant voice seemed to carry all over the camp, and she looked around warily. But just as she started to climb, he dropped his precious flute, grasped the branch he was sitting on, fell backwards until he was hanging by his knees, and flipped out of the tree. He somersaulted down the path.

Forgetting her desire for secrecy, she picked up the flute and followed behind him.

"Stop your foolishness, Onan. Wait for me. I need to talk with you." When she was out of breath, she stopped and placed her hands on her hips. "You are not a child any more, Onan. You're a grown man about to be married, and you can't act like this anymore."

Hunched over with his face between his legs, Onan stopped. "Married. Married to who? Who-who-who?" He didn't look at her, but gazed at the pebbles on the path.

"To Tamar, of course." She dropped the flute. "Onan, don't you understand? Don't you know anything?"

"Yes...I know Tamar. Tamar is Er's wife; Er's beautiful, beautiful wife. Beautiful, beautiful Tamar. I played my flute for them at the marriage feast and everybody looked for me." He giggled. "But nobody found me. Nobody but Tamar. Clever, clever Tamar. She looked right up into my tree. Right up, right up." The finger he extended pointed at the ground due to his position.

Ruah jerked him upright and held his cheeks in her fingertips. "Er is dead now, Onan, and they want to make Tamar your wife. Yours, you understand me, not Er's." As she spoke, her thumbs jerked his head back and forth.

"Er is dead. Tamar is mine. Beautiful, beautiful Tamar is mine. Mine-mine-mine-mine..."

"No! We've got to stop them, Onan, for your sake. You and me together. They want to kill you just as they killed my poor Er. They took my precious husband before he could even see his baby." She patted her belly, and then turned back to him with clenched fists. "It's all her fault. She is as evil as Astarte is. If she hadn't come here and bewitched Er, none of this would have happened, and Er and I would still be happily married."

As her hands came up to cover her sobs, Onan grabbed his flute and flip-flopped his way back to his tree. She stomped to the foot of the tree, but her efforts to stop the stream of notes that poured forth from the flute like an intoxicating wine availed little. Finally she walked away, discouraged but determined to try again as many times as necessary to win him. Tamar had to die and with her, her lover, the evil Master.

The early darkness of the winter solstice descended over the camp. A storm lashed at the tent walls, thumping at Ashuah's needlework with the persistence of a reveler's drum. Yet the tent was dry, and full to the seams with Judah's family, friends, servants and slaves. Children huddled in their mother's bosoms, cringing at every boom of thunder while his men were served their choice of wine or goat milk. Though the group was divided, the men on Judah's side of the tent, and the women and small children on the other, the division was a bit more informal than was general with his people, and he himself sat in the opening between the two sides where both groups could see him.

The Little One sat in the far corner by herself with her needlework. She had rebuffed his friendship since their talk about her marriage to Onan. She was angry with him, but what could he do? It was the law, and besides, he could not very well make her his own wife now, could he? Ashuah had taken Er's death better than he expected, but Er was her son, and Tamar was involved in his death.

Onan lounged at his left, fingering his flute without making a sound on it. Twice Ruah had gestured to draw him further to the back of the tent, but he had ignored her hushed entreaties. As usual on these occasions, everyone clamored for a different story.

"Tell us of the giants, Master Judah."

"No, of old Noah."

"How about the pillar of salt?"

Judah patted his son's knee. "And what would you like to hear first, Onan? You are the soon-to-be-groom. What is your favorite?"

Onan continued to stare upwards. Finally, he replied in his high-pitched tones while his hands swooped the flute up and down like a dove searching for an olive branch. "Abba, I would be a bird, and soar, soar, soar. Tell us of the sparrow, and how he saved man, how, how, how."

Judah chuckled at Onan's love of sounds and held out his arms to receive his youngest son, Shelah, a ritual he always followed when he told stories. It sometimes seemed to him the only time he could publicly hold his sons and play with them without appearing foolish. As he began to talk, the tiny hands pulled on his beard and explored his ear, but what did that matter?

"As long as you remember, my sons, that this is a tale told by widows when the babes are pulling at her tunic and she has wicks to trim and lentils to shell, not a history of truth as are most of my other stories."

Everyone nodded encouragingly. They had heard the mock warning many times before. It seemed to him they enjoyed the imagined stories more than truth. While he cleared his throat, Ashuah hushed the children. He pretended to be trying to remember where to begin until the little ones prompted him.

"The garden."

"Adam."

"The snake."

"Ah, yes. That was where it was. It was at the time when Adam and Eve first left the garden that the sparrow got his forked tail. He had not been injured in a fall. Oh no, he lost it by saving mankind and making it possible for you and me to be here together listening to Yah talk to us in the blessed winter rain and thunder while we stay safe and warm and dry in our tent."

Shelah stuck his fingers in his father's mouth and examined the points of his teeth. With hardly a pause, Judah moved the chubby digits back to his ear. "It was, of course, the serpent who caused all the fuss. He was angry that Yah had commanded him to stay away from the couple and crawl away on his belly like that pitiful creature, the worm, so he demanded an audience before Yah to plead his case."

He tried to capture the eyes of the Little One across the room, but she was as distant to him as Yah had seemed these many years.

"'If I am not allowed to go near the couple, I will surely starve to death,' the serpent argued. 'I will be removed from the numbering of creation, for my food is as theirs. What would you have me do?' he appealed. 'Is the soil itself the fruit of my temptation?' And he bit a huge bite of dirt to see if this was what Yah had in mind."

Reaching down, he pretended to put a handful of dirt into his own mouth, which he could not have done even if he wanted to for the many layers of mats that covered the ground. He heaved and made choking noises until his eyes actually watered and many other eyes were wet with laughter.

The Little One did not laugh and neither did Ashuah. "'Ah....ah...I think this is not it,' the serpent told Yah with his gritty voice, and he lay down heaving and shaking; trying to get the dirt through his long, long body as soon as possible. His misery touched the heart of Yah, and He proclaimed, 'I will send out a creature to find for you the tastiest food in all of my creation, and that will be your food from this day forth.'"

When Shelah reached over and pulled on his brother's short curls, Onan took the baby's hand and sat up. How many years had it been since his eyes had met those of his son as they did now? Judah grinned.

"Immediately the serpent stopped his shaking, for it was a bit put on, you see, and demanded Yah's oath that no matter what the creature said, Yah would not break his promise. Yah called forth a tiny gnat. 'Here is your creature,' he pronounced. 'Let him taste of all creation and declare the most delicious food.'"

Judah's eyes involuntarily traveled back to the forlorn figure huddled in the corner and then back again to his son. "Now even before the gnat had left on his gluttonous mission, the serpent had attempted to convince him that it was unnecessary, that he already knew what the best food was: a man or a woman, or better yet, a tender baby boy."

As he said this, Judah lifted Shelah high up in the air and jiggled him until the baby laughed.

Seth, a three year old who, in a few years, would have all the mischievousness of the infamous Joshua of Chezib, came up to him and tapped him on his arm. Judah fully expected anything from a request for Judah to go with him to relieve himself or even a command to be quiet and let him tell the story, but Seth was only anxious to know when he was going to get to the sparrow. Deciding that what he really wanted was to fly like a sparrow as Shelah had done, Judah took one hand and lifted Seth quickly up and then down. Suddenly children surrounded him and the story was forgotten for the moment. Finally, meeting the eyes of Onan for the second time this evening, Judah met his mute request with a nod. *Say goodbye to childhood, my son.* Judah lifted Onan high above him.

After having given all the children and older boys at least three "flights," he was finally able to return to the story. "It was on his way back to report to Yah that indeed the serpent had been right and people were the best food that the gnat met the sparrow, and the sparrow was able to get him to confess his report. But as he said, 'people are the best food, people are the best food,' the sparrow drew nearer and nearer to him until he jumped up and pecked off the gnat's tongue, and the last time it came out 'people are tzzz'."

Seth led several of the smaller children romping around the room with their tongues stuck out imitating "people are tzzzz....tzzzz....tzzzz." This time Onan accompanied their frolic with a melody on his flute, but showed no signs of wanting to join them. Perhaps he had indeed said his goodbye to childhood. Without any sign from Judah, Seth made all the children sit in relative quiet so he could hear the end of the story.

"When Yah appeared, the sparrow told Him that the gnat had met with an accident, but that before it had happened, he had given him his report and that the best food in the world for a serpent was frogs. 'Then frogs it shall be,' Yah proclaimed. Adam and Eve were so happy that they hugged and kissed each other, but the serpent was so angry he jumped up and tried to kill the sparrow right there in front of Yah." As the children jumped up and down, some pretending to be gnats and others frogs, Judah reached out and tickled their stomachs as if he was the serpent trying to get them. "But all the serpent got was a mouth full of tail feathers." He held up his empty hand and made little spitting noises.

His mouth was indeed dry from so much frivolity, and he asked for the wineskin to be passed to him before he could begin a more serious story.

Chapter 12

The Festival of the Shepherds, when she would be given to Onan, was fast approaching. Tamar busied herself with her weaving and tried not to think of it. There would be no feast in their honor this time. Onan would simply move into her tent and take her.

She shuddered. Not that Onan was ugly or repulsive; often, when he played his delightful melodies or curled himself up in a strange kind of knot and rolled down the hill, he made her eyes shine with laughter, as they had not done since she was a small child. She worried that he so often cut or bruised himself in these outlandish displays. In a way, that was the problem. She could easily see herself mothering this child-who-was-not-a-child for the rest of her life... but as his wife, what would he want of her?

"What are you contemplating so sadly, Little One?"

Tamar looked up. The Master was standing over her, watching her intertwine the yellow threads of the sunlight through the browns and greens already on the loom. She tied a knot and bit off the excess thread. "My marriage. Master, I am sorry for the way I have been acting toward you. I know you only did what you thought best."

When he made a slight nod and cleared his throat, she took it for an acceptance of her apology. "Master, I have been wondering if I might cut holes in my tent sides to let in the sunlight like our windows at home. Once I am married, it will not be proper to leave the entire tent flap up all day as I do now."

"But if you cut holes in your tent, the rain will come in, and you will become sick."

"Not if I sew a piece of skin to the top of the hole and roll it up to be lowered only when it rains. It needn't be a large opening, only about a span wide and two spans high. I just need some sunlight to brighten my tent."

He paced the tent from end to end and chewed on his thumbnail. "It is your tent, Little One. Do as seems best to you."

He came back and sat on his haunches beside her. "I came to tell you a surprise. I took your advice and sent for a slave to teach Onan the art of writing. He will be here within a few weeks."

She rushed to thank him, but his face reddened and he held her away from him. As she withdrew her hands and cast her eyes to the ground, he mumbled, "I will send a servant to help you with the windows."

Then he walked away.

The wedding night passed without event—any event at all. Servants moved Onan's things into her tent, and she had lain shivering under her blanket waiting for him to come to her.

However, he did not. Somehow, he had gotten into the tent on his side without her seeing him. He played his flute at intervals throughout the night, but he never visited her bed or called for her to come to him.

Towards dawn, she slept. Strange dreams haunted her of Onan playing his flute to call up the serpent to cut out her tongue. She was dressed in brightly colored feathers and they were so hot that they made her itch all over. She looked up to see Onan in his tree wildly playing his flute and laughing as he watched her run from the serpent. She ran as fast as she could, but the serpent kept getting closer and closer. Yet he wasn't running as she was; he was dancing, moving his lithe coil to the rhythm of the flute. The shimmering snake wrapped itself around her leg and slithered up between her breasts. She screamed.

A hand cupped over her mouth and smothered the scream. "Are you trying to bring the evil master up here to comfort the loveless bride?"

Tamar opened her eyes. Ruah was bending over her.

"I doubt even he would find you very attractive with your sweat smeared cosmetics and that tangled mass of hair." Ruah removed her large hand from Tamar's mouth.

"What are you doing here, Ruah? I didn't send for anyone." She was tired and wanted to bathe, and wished to end this encounter as swiftly as possible.

Ruah seemed in no hurry to go. "No one sends for me anymore. I am no longer a slave. Remember that." She folded her hands across her belly. "I came to help clean up the wedding night mess." She snickered. "But I see there isn't any."

You came to spy. "You forget that I am a widow, Ruah, and have no need to prove anything to anyone. No matter what you may think you know; you know nothing." She stood to face the girl. "Now, please leave my tent."

"I know Onan never lay with you last night, and if I have anything to say about it, he never will."

As she watched Ruah leave, Tamar did not know what to think. Had Ruah unknowingly helped her, or was she plotting more evil? Ruah hated her and the Master enough to try anything. But what of Onan? Would Ruah hurt Onan to get to them?

Many times over the next several days, Tamar felt Onan watching her. He would enter and leave the tent from somewhere on his side, but when he was gone from the tent, she could never find the place of his entrance, and when he was there, she never dared look. Even when she knew he was there, she could never catch his eyes looking directly at her; they were always staring up to the blackness of the tent roof. Twice she saw Onan's hand slip under his tunic as he stared at the blackness, and the white of his seed as it stained his clothing. However, she felt his eyes as she taught the young servants the art of weaving, as she bent over the iron oven or cooking pots, and as she bathed the desert sweat from her body.

She could not rid herself of the fear that gripped her as she thought of her unnatural marriage. She should be glad of the reprieve from the violence that men such as Er and Ben Qara forced on their women, but her few moments with the Master showed her that it did not have to be that way.

Chapter 13

Tamar held up the blanket she was working on to show the two young slaves she was teaching. "You see, Sheba, you must keep the pressure of your hand steadier when you spin so that your thread does not make lumps you do not desire in your work."

The girls gazed at the work. Sheba pointed at one corner. "It looks like the night sky, Mistress. I can see the moon and the stars over the mountaintop."

Tamar frowned. This time she had deliberately tried not to put any pattern at all in the weaving, merely to lighten the darkness of the blue with specks of white. "Do you see that too, Kisse?"

The younger girl giggled and nodded. She ran to the open window flap and stared out at the view of the mountaintop. "Perhaps, Mistress, you looked out the hole in your tent without knowing it, and wove into your work the beauty of the heavens."

"Yah forgive me!" Tamar threw down the accursed piece. She went to get the chopping axe from beside the oven to destroy the wretched thing. *Mother never had this problem with her blankets.* Everyone saw an image in her work, but it was their own image, not that of their neighbor.

"No, Mistress, please don't destroy it. I will take it from your sight if it displeases you, but do not ruin it." Tears flowed down Kisse's cheeks as though it would be her fault if the blanket were destroyed because she had seen what was not intended to be there. "Why would a good God like Yah desire you to destroy such beauty, Mistress?"

Tamar sank to the floor, dropping the axe beside her. "I don't know why, Kisse." She sighed. "Sometimes the ways of Yah cannot be understood by His children; they are only meant to be obeyed." Wiping her moist eyes, she gathered up the blanket. "Let us take this to the Master. He will decide."

The night was far advanced when Tamar finally returned to the tent. There had been so much to do today. It was the last night of the Festival of the Shepherds, the night of the full moon. The Master had slaughtered the young goat, and everyone in the camp had partaken a small portion of it. The men had lifted up endless prayers. After spending the afternoon helping the Mistress prepare and clean up, she was tired and eager to go to her bed.

Tamar was immediately aware that she was not alone in the tent. Though the lamp was not lit, the moon shone through the open window, spreading its light over much of her half but leaving the edges in darkness. As she crept further into the tent, she nearly tripped over a corner of her newest weaving. One of the girls must have returned it to the tent after the Master gave his permission. But why had they spread it across the floor? She started to pick it up, but a tiny sound made her drop the blanket and peer into the darkness. She could hardly whisper. "Onan, are you there?"

She moved into the middle of the room. A halo of moonlight encircled her head and spread itself over her like a veil of white linen. He could easily see her if he was present, but he did not come forth.

She worked up the courage to speak a bit louder. "Onan, where are you?" Her heart pounded faster with each step. "Will you not speak to me, my husband?"

The laughter that came from beside the center partition did little to ease her fear. "Speak? Speak, speak, speak...How shall I speak?"

"What do you mean, Onan? Why could you not speak to me? I am your wife." He might not have heard her. He continued as if he did not.

"How dare I to speak to Astarte, Mother of the moon, who commands the moon and the stars to bow at her feet?"

Tamar was quaking. She kicked at the blanket under her feet, and spoke as harshly as possible to hide her fear. "Do not talk nonsense, Onan. This is only a blanket. One I intend to destroy immediately."

The high-pitched voice from the darkness ceased its fearsome laughter and commanded in a voice so unlike that of Onan that she had to believe him when he said, "No. Astarte must not take away the lights. I am not Onan. Onan is gone. Gone to be with Yah. I am Baal, husband of Astarte."

Tamar covered her ears and shook her head wildly. "No, do not say such wicked things. You must be Onan."

The voice took on a softer pleading quality. "Astarte will love Baal, for Baal is the priest of Astarte. Er was not a good priest, for he did not bring Astarte her gift. Baal would not want children for Er. Er was a bad priest."

Her hands came down and cradled her throat. "I don't know what you're talking about, Onan. I don't need any gifts. I am not Astarte. I am Tamar, your wife."

The voice continued in the same strange tone. "I have brought her gift so Astarte will not destroy the lights. A gift to lay on the iron altar of fire."

"Whatever do you mean? I have no iron altar, Onan, only an oven to cook you food on." She was weary of the struggle she could not win. "What have you done? Come out and tell me."

As he stepped from the shadows, she saw that he had covered himself with his own blood. In his right hand he held the bloodied chopping axe, and in the left...

He had castrated himself.

Covering her mouth, Tamar ran outside. When she had vomited the contents of the large evening meal, she ran down the hillside screaming wildly for the Master and Mistress.

"He is dying," Judah said bluntly to Tamar when he came out of her tent. "We cannot stop the bleeding. What happened here?"

Tamar shook her head. "I do not know, Master. Onan was talking wildly. He said I was Astarte and he was Baal, and he had a gift for me. He tossed it to the ground at my feet." She began to cry again.

Judah resisted the urge to put his arm around her and comfort her. "Why would my son think you Astarte?"

She gulped. "The moon shone brightly through my window, Master, and…and he had spread that wretched blanket across the floor. He said even the moon and the stars had to bow at my feet."

Judah's mind recalled another dream, Joseph's dream. Would Yah never be finished punishing him?

Ashuah lifted the black tent flap. "Our second son is dead."

Chapter 14

Oni reached Tamar's tent as the Mistress delivered the news. The calm was as dreadful as the stagnant air after a sirocco wind had passed. No one screamed or fainted. No one seemed to have the energy to do so. No one pointed a finger accusingly. They stood so still so long, he felt urged to shake them to be certain Yah had not made them into pillars of salt in an overflow of his wrath. Finally, the Master lifted his hands with an almost ceremonious deliberateness and ripped his linen tunic from top to bottom. Then the women did the same. The Mistress turned to go back in to the body of her son and the Master descended the hill to his own tent, leaving the Little One to fall into a heap by the tent flap. She covered her face with clumps of long hair and wept.

Oni stood undecided for a while, and then turned to fetch Deborah. She would be more help with the women. He would go to Master Judah, his friend whom most thought so cold, but who he knew was hurting to the depths of his spirit. The boy Onan had always been a bit strange. Master Judah had said it was boyish foolishness, but Oni had never been certain. He sighed and ripped the linen tunic Deborah had made for him especially for the Festival of the Shepherds, his first festal garment as a free man entitled to its fine linen embroidery.

By the time he had awakened Deborah, acquainted her with the night's tragedy, and sent her to the Little One's tent loaded with provisions for the burial preparations, Oni felt fully the weight of his years.

When he entered the Master's tent, Judah was already shaving off his beard with a sharpened dagger. His face was hairless on one side, and all but one patch was missing from the other.

"Come in, Oni. I will be finished in a moment." The sharp blade passed ruthlessly across that final patch, sending the shorn hairs flying to the ground.

Oni watched them fall. Deborah would be so angry with him if he let his hair drop to the floor that way. It was so hard to separate from the goat hair mats. He knelt and gathered the hair with the blade of his knife. "How may I serve you, Master?"

Judah lifted the dagger and held its point with the tip of his left forefinger. "You could tell me what I have done wrong in raising my sons, my friend. That is what I most need to know."

"I am a poor choice to ask of your failings as a parent, Master. After all, my daughter was joined in guilt to your son." He carried the pile of hair to the tent flap for the wind to carry away.

"But why have they done such evil, Oni? Were they punished for my sin against my brother by receiving an evil spirit?"

The Master was distraught, and his wild gestures brought the sharp point of the dagger often perilously close to them both.

"No, Master, I do not believe that." He calmly took the dagger from the Master's clenched fingers at the first opportunity. The Master stared at his hand dully. "Their sin was their own, and it was more than enough to merit Yah's wrath. You did well to teach your sons to follow the ways of Yah. That they did not, that they listened to the ways of the Canaanite gods, Yah will not hold to your account."

He dropped the dagger to the floor and held the Master to his chest as he had done many times when Judah was a small boy.

The night had been long. The small body of Onan was packed with myrrh and other spices between layers and layers of white linen. He was ready for burial, but he yet lay on the mat on his side of the tent. The smell of death already invaded Tamar's nostrils.

A storm was gathering, and the wind beat against the tent. The covering of the little window was lowered, never to be raised again. As she pulled the heavy black veil down over her darkened eyes, she determined never to lift it in the sight of another man. Er had called her a hierodule; Onan, Astarte. How had she, who had never worshipped anyone but the true God, Yah, been used to lead two young men of the *Habiri* to their destruction? It must be her face. There was no other answer for it. Her face was despised in the sight of Yah, a tool of evil. She touched every part of the face with her fingertips as if memorizing it.

The wind beat the veil to the contours of her face as she came out of the tent and sought to breathe the storm-freshened air. A hellish quiet blanketed the camp. The Shepherd's celebration was forgotten as slaves lay by their tents or walked silently up the path with their eyes determinedly lowered as they passed her. When baby Shelah reached out a pudgy hand to her, the young slave carrying him grasped it and ran with him back to the Mistress's tent as if her touch would send him also to join his brothers in the cold tomb. Stricken, Tamar lifted her arms to the wind and cried out to Yah for mercy.

"At the death of my son Er, you convinced me, my husband, the she bore no blame, but surely you can't say that Onan had any malice in him. There was never a more gentle soul born on this earth." Ashuah paced to relieve her anger, but it did not abate.

"No, no he was not evil as Er was, but he did an evil thing. A thing Yah would not forgive. We should never have married him to Tamar. He was still so much like a little child. He was not ready to be a husband." Judah sat with his feet crossed up under him at the ankles and rocked.

"She created an image, which you know Yah doesn't like, and Onan paid the price," Ashuah accused.

"What would you have me to do to her?"

Ashuah could hardly hear Judah. "Send her forth from here. Back to her father. Back to the trader. I do not care."

"Is she then guilty of our son's sins?" His quiet voice fed her rage.

"Why do you defend her?" She shouted and didn't care that it was not respectful. "Was Ruah truthful in her words against you?"

He sighed, shaking his head. He ran his fingers through the curls at the back of his head. "If she is guilty, then I am also, for I saw the blanket and found no harm in it."

"You had your mind on the preparations for the Festival of the Shepherds and did not look at it properly." She had no wish to blame him. It was the girl's fault.

Judah shook his head. "No. I saw it. Would you send me away also?"

Tamar came through the tent flap just then. "No, Master. The Mistress is right. I should go. As soon as we have buried my husband tomorrow, I will return to the house of my father." She turned to Ashuah. "Mistress, please believe me. I am so sorry to have brought you pain."

Ashuah stared at the blackness of the tent wall. "How have you come to listen at my tent? I see Ruah was right. You have many evil ways."

"No, please do not think that. I only came to ask if a place might be found for me to stay the night. The stink of death is strong in the tent."

Ashuah glared at her with contempt. "I will find a place."

The mourners followed the path up the mountainside. Slaves carried the litter with the body of Onan. Other slaves could be seen at the tomb shoving at the heavy stone that covered the mouth of the cave. The funereal lament resounded in Judah's ears. The storm had passed and the sky was cloudless, but the heavy rain had made the path muddy and often the procession had to stop as one of the litter carriers slipped.

When they reached the entrance, Judah moved ahead of the slaves to be the first to enter the tomb. Once he had passed through the entrance he could stand upright, at least until he reached the inner chamber where Er's body already lay on the cold stone. He could not look at the body of his oldest son as he motioned for the slaves to bring in the second. The myrrh-mixed death smell filled his nostrils. He busied himself checking the smaller rocks that supported the narrow stone beds.

As he watched the great stone roll back into place over the opening, Judah covered his head with his prayer shawl and lifted up his hands. He still stood that way when the afternoon sun was high in the sky and one of the young boys of the camp reported a caravan cresting the mountaintop. By the time Judah reached the camp, Hirah had passed the unruly camels to his slaves and was sitting surrounded by the children of the camp. Children always loved Hirah not only for the small gifts he had for them, but simply because he talked with them, really talked. Onan had especially....

"My friend, I have heard the news." Hirah arose to greet Judah.

"No, you must not come near me, Hirah. I am unclean."

"Nonsense, my friend," Hirah retorted. "I respect your God because He is your God, but I will gladly be unclean if I can comfort my friend." Before Judah could object, Hirah had bear hugged him, and Judah did indeed feel comforted.

As they sat before the tent, Hirah told Judah of his travels through the lands of Babylon and the Chaldeans. He had brought back the promised slave as well as many rich foods and spices to tempt the sternest palate. He described marvelous inventions to make the water come to the farmer that his labor might be lessened and his harvest strong. Judah listened, but he did not hear. At least not at first. However, in his usual gentle way, Hirah gave light to his darkness and finally Judah was able to speak of the tragedy that had befallen his family since their last meeting. After much persuasion, Hirah finally consented to take the Little One back to her family in Chezib. First, of course, he offered to marry her himself to prove her virtue, but Judah would not allow it.

By law, he said, she was betrothed to Shelah. Her virtue was not in question.

END OF BOOK ONE

Book Two

Chapter 7

Shelah remembered the tales his father, Judah, had told of the poverty of the town of Chezib, and Father had visited here during the richness of feast times! Now the years of drought and famine had left little of the tiny town. The dust-coated hawthorn scrub gave evidence where the wall had once been, but Shelah could not find a trace of it still standing. As he picked his way through the rubble that might have been the gateway, he paused to take a long gulp from his wineskin.

The village was incredibly quiet. No bazaar, not even a single merchant sat in one of the deserted booths that lined the square. The palm branch roofs rested, for the most part, on no more than three posts, and waited for that one strong wind that would put them to rest permanently. No children ran back and forth shouting their loud jeering challenges to the younger ones who had not yet proved themselves. As he wandered, Shelah could see no one at all who could tell him the house he sought.

The paths were wide. Many of the mud-brick houses had disintegrated completely, leaving only mounds of dust, which were scattered by the wind from pile to pile, filling the air with their coarse grain. Evidence that many people had once lived here was everywhere. Clay lamps and butter pots littered the paths. Dyes spilled over and painted the dirt along the edge of a few houses. And bones. It seemed like everywhere he looked, there were bones. That had to be a donkey, those perhaps a lamb, but those...he shuddered and bit his lower lip. Perhaps he had been foolish to insist he must make the journey from Adullam alone. Father would be so angry when he returned from his food-buying trip to Egypt. Oni and Hirah had both tried to warn him how it was here, but he had not listened. He'd had no idea.

Though a slight breeze blew through the empty streets, it had no cooling effect. It seemed to push his hot breath back into his face. He gave an involuntary yelp as he spied the well, in spite of his certainty that it would be dry. It was. Dust had filled the cavity and made the large ring of rocks only a lip on a shallow bowl. Wearily he sat on one of the rocks, shaking the sand from his loose sandals.

At first, he thought her only a mirage, a blur of darkness in the glare of the sunlight, but he felt almost immediately that it could truly only be Tamar. More than once when his Father wasn't around, Oni had told him the sad story of the lovely young woman who still hid herself beneath the heavy layers of black veiling after all these years of widowhood. Other widows might remain in the town, but surely they would not veil themselves so completely in this dreadful heat.

Oni said it was a shame so many people felt so much guilt about two boys not worth the emotion. Though blunt of speech, the brusque old man was as beloved to him as his own father, and he trusted his assessment of Er and Onan's character more than those who would lighten the boys' guilt by shouldering so much of it themselves.

"Tamar. Please wait. Tamar!"

The mirage ceased retreating. Shelah returned his shoe to his foot and ran toward her. She stood so still he instantly connected her with his father's tales of Lot's wife, though she had not looked back at him. The black wool shroud engulfed all of her but her eyes. As he reached her, he was almost panting for breath because of the heat, but he dared not lower his eyes for even an instant lest she disappear.

As he held her gaze, he knew at once that she was still as beautiful as she could have ever been, even if she did hide it beneath all that swathing. How could one possibly describe those deep brown eyes? The only thing that came to mind almost made him laugh: sun-dusty ripe olives. Enos would laugh at that. He always said that Shelah had no imagination at all when it came to description. Enos was the slave who had been his teacher ever since he could remember, but much more than that, he was his friend. Enos would say something romantic, like her eyes were wells in the midst of the desert.

Shelah held back his hand, though he wanted to reach out and touch her quivering shoulder. He smiled. "Please do not be frightened of me. I would not hurt you, truly."

The crack of his voice betrayed more nervousness than he had expected to feel. To cover his embarrassment, he covered his eyes for only a moment. She turned away.

"You are much more the image of your father than were your brothers."

The strength of her voice surprised him, considering the trembling that shook her veils.

"More than just his image. I am more my father than were Er and Onan." He wasn't sure exactly why he deliberately called his brothers by name. He had no wish to be cruel to her, but perhaps he did wish to test Oni's opinion in some way.

Oni was right. The power of Yah was strong in her. It was as if the mere mention of their names brought Him down like a shield around her. The shivering stopped, and her shoulders straightened.

Her eyes again met his. "I hope you speak the truth, Young Master...for your sake."

The words could have been a threat if they had not been so gently spoken.

"Take me to your father, Mistress. I must speak with him." His sun-roughened hand touched her tiny pale, work-wrinkled one peeping from the shroud. He felt the birth of a bond of trust between them. Perhaps.

She turned again without a word and descended toward the wide street. He hurried to catch up with her. He had often raced Enos in the evenings to pass time, and he was never considered slow. Why, then, was it so difficult to keep up with a woman hampered by layers and layers of cloth? Did she move on the feet of angels, or were his own feet slowed with dread of the task set before him?

The house she entered was not the small hut he had expected from Oni's account of their first visit to Chezib. It was a large masonry home with a faded red dome roof on it. It was not far at all from the well. In fact, it seemed to be the only house in the town still safe enough to enter. She ignored the stairs along the wall leading to the arched doorways of the upper rooms, and plunged into the semi-darkness of the columned hallway that led to the inner courtyard. He lost his guide as he stopped to touch one of the delicately sculpted pillars, but soon he saw her silhouetted in the courtyard archway. He squinted as he entered the courtyard's sunlight.

Protected by the house from the worst of the heat and wind, and obviously tended with loving care by the inhabitants, the garden was a tiny bit of Eden. Dark green vines such as he had never seen before entwined sculpted posts. A milky fur came off in his hands when he brushed them. In the very center of the court, a giant date palm bowed its offerings within his easy reach, and he did not hesitate to pluck the plump, inviting fruit. The thick pulp was sweet and juicy though it was still early summer, and most of the harvest elsewhere was not yet ripe. In the shade of the gnarled base, bronze pots of bright orange flowers burst forth their exotic blooms and scented the air with a dizzying freshness; all growing abundantly as if there were no lack of water in Chezib.

Tamar stood back in the shadows for a while as if allowing him to drink his fill at an oasis. She then moved over to a barrel and handed him a cup of the coolest, sweetest wine he had drunk in a long time. "How...?"

"Hirah," she said simply.

"Of course." It was the only explanation. His father's gentle friend who traveled all over the world bringing back the most wonderful treasures, and often, instead of selling the best of them, giving them to his friends. Only he could make the desert bloom in the midst of this fearsome drought.

He had to remind himself of his errand. "Your father?"

She pointed him toward the far side of the courtyard. Again, his eyes had to focus on the shadows, and he was startled. On three black couches facing him lay three gaunt figures. On the far right, an ancient woman with long silver hair and skin that seemed too tight to cover her prominent cheekbones. She appeared to be sleeping soundly. A steady snore emanated from her beaklike nose, and he wondered how he had failed to hear it before. On the far left, an old man with an almost bald head and a scruffy beard nearly as long as the old woman's hair. The man stared out at the courtyard. Occasionally, he bleated out a sound something like "shoes."

But it was the man in the middle who held Shelah's attention. Although at least as old as the other two, he was wide-awake, his eyes focused on Shelah. Shelah was certain that if he made one mistake in his dealings with the girl, this man would bring him to account for it. The ancient figure sat up straight and peered at him with stony eyes. He gasped and pointed his bony finger.

"And have you come at last to claim my daughter as your brothers did?" The effort appeared too much for him, and he fell back onto his pillowed chaise.

At least the Man of God's mind was clear. He had not mistaken Shelah for his father, and he did not live in the past, as the other man seemed to do. Shelah praised Yah for that. The aged priest deserved an answer. Shelah took a deep breath.

"No, Sir, I have not. I have come to release her from her bond to me."

Chapter 2

Benu'el relaxed. At last, Yah had sent the strong young ally he had prayed for these many years. But first, he must be tested.

"And why would you release her from this bond?" he demanded. His stern voice still had the ability to intimidate those who would lie to him, but the boy did not appear frightened. Respectful yes, but not frightened. He liked that.

"I cannot marry someone who is already married to another, Sir," the lad answered simply. "It is against the will of Yah."

Narrowing his eyes, Benu'el raised himself up on his elbows. "Then you believe the nonsense your brother spoke?"

He reached for the oak cane that rested beside his couch. The boy shook his head, but did not back up, or even blink.

"I did not mean that at all, Sir. I meant no disrespect to my father, or to your daughter. I only meant that your daughter claims my father's soul. He cries out her name in his sleep, and he wakes up cold with sweat night after night."

Benu'el could not help the satisfaction that quivered through him. For years he had blamed himself that he had blindly followed Yah's instructions when he had left the town that day, only to have the man that Yah had selected disclaim the relationship. "You do know what your brother claimed then?"

Hesitating only momentarily, the boy nodded. "I know Father stayed the night with her, and I believe he would have taken her, but Oni arrived too soon with the news of my birth. Had Er been speaking the truth, Father would have never given your daughter to him. That much I know."

"And do you know the rest of the story also?" Benu'el glanced over at old Emi who could sleep through thunder, and now spent most of her days filling the room with the thunder of her snoring. Then over at Samuel, his cousin who, though younger than Benu'el, no longer cared about the future or even the present, but spent his days in the time he was still a small boy hawking shoes at his father's bazaar stand. Their knowledge of Tamar's fate in Hebron would no longer help or hurt her.

For her sake, or so he had always told himself, he had fought desperately to keep it secret these many years. How well he had succeeded, he could never be certain. People had often stared at her in the town after her return, but he had always believed that was because of those accursed veils she insisted on hiding under. He had demanded she tell no one of her disgrace. He was certain she had obeyed. But she cried. Often, alone in the night, he still heard her weep. How could he not be glad when he heard from the son that the father also suffered in the night from his prideful absence from the one he had called "Little One"?

The lad's voice broke his reverie. "Yes, I know it."

"All of it?" Benu'el was surprised. He had thought Judah would have guarded his shame as carefully as had Benu'el.

"How can one ever be sure of that?" The boy absently fingered the date seed he still held. Finally, he tossed it into a pile of seeds by the post. "I think so. I was eager to know the truth so that I might not make the same mistakes my brothers did. However, if you worry that it is common knowledge, you worry in vain. I put together little pieces from those involved. As the chronicler of my family history, no one is the least surprised when I ask questions. I do it all the time about everyone." He grinned, and picked at the scarlet sleeve of his cloak. "It is a great deal of work to be what my father calls a 'Man of Leisure'."

Benu'el heard a light laugh behind him. It had been many years since he had heard that laugh. He held up his wrinkled hand to be taken by his daughter. "What lightens your heart, my child?"

Emerging from the shadows, she knelt beside him. "Only that the Master must have indeed changed that he would allow his son to be a man of leisure. He always demanded that his sons must work equally."

The boy looked a little red, and shuffled his feet slightly. He was so young, a mere lad trying desperately to be a man. He would be a good man though, an honest one even when it hurt. He rubbed his hands over his bare chin and up into his curly brown hair, looking sympathetically down at the kneeling figure.

"I'm afraid that was at my mother's insistence, Mistress. She was afraid I would be hurt tending to the sheep as Onan often was." He squatted. "My father has changed from what I am told he was like when you knew him, but I doubt that you would be happy with the difference."

Feeling suddenly cold, Benu'el reached to cover himself with the blanket of the chaise. Accursed black cloth: on the blanket, on his tunic, and on her. That's all the woman would weave. It was such a waste, such a sin against Yah. "Your father has changed? How?"

The boy seemed to be hesitating over whether or where to sit. Benu'el moved his feet aside, and motioned him to sit on the end of the chaise. At his nod, Shelah sat. He sighed.

"My father is a very religious man, but his religion is empty, as if he is certain that Yah has left him, but by pretending His continued presence he can make Him return. Is that possible? I mean, can one call up Yah just by reciting lines so many times a day for so many years?"

The innocent eyes stared helplessly into Benu'el's tired ones. Here was Benu'el's successor: the one who would carry on his task in instructing the people in the true ways of Yah.

"Bring out my mantle, Tamar." He lay back on his chaise with his eyes closed until she returned with it. The boy must have thought him asleep, for he moved back into the courtyard and walked from plant to plant examining the fragrant blooms and odd shaped leaves. Benu'el smiled.

"Here it is, Father." As he sat up again, she wrapped the mantle around his shoulders, and Benu'el fingered it lovingly. Elsbeth had made it for him not long after their marriage. 'A mantle worthy a prophet' she had called it, and it still was. Its white linen was embroidered with scarlet and gold in swirls and loops, and somehow just wearing it always gave him assurance of the nearness of Yah, and of His power.

The boy returned and stood at the foot of his chaise.

"Your father must be made to carry out his responsibility to my daughter. You have abdicated any rights before me, and before Samuel." He ignored the fact that Samuel had no realization that the boy was even present, much less that he was abdicating any rights.

"Take off your shoe." Shelah glanced at him questioningly, but did as he was bidden. "Shake it out as a symbol of your abandoning any claim to my daughter."

Laying his hand atop the clasped hands of Tamar and her father, Shelah vigorously denied it. "But I do not abandon claim to her. I claim her as my sister, and demand that she in truth be my stepmother as soon as possible." With these words he then shook the leather thong with so much energy that dust flew from the seemingly clean sandal.

"Now." With trembling fingers, Benu'el removed the mantle from his shoulders. "Every prophet needs a son in the faith, and I have waited many years for you to appear. Come closer, that I may bless you."

With his sandal still in hand, Shelah knelt, and Benu'el kissed him on the forehead. "Tamar, bring me some oil."

As carefully as his arthritic fingers would allow, he glided the white linen across the scholar's scarlet cloak. The tiny cup of oil Tamar handed him wetted Shelah's wiry curls without spilling a drop onto the precious mantle.

"A double portion of Yah's Spirit, I would bequeath to this, my son in the faith. Yah, make him more fruitful than I, that because of his children's children, many would seek Your face." Exhausted, he lay back; enjoying the first peace he had felt in a long time.

Chapter 3

Shelah returned the sandal to his foot, and stood speechless for a time. Finally, as he fingered the linen, it was as if he could feel the power of a priest, the power of Yah, grow within him. "Now, I would see the face of the sister I have never seen."

But as he reached to draw aside the black cloth, Tamar drew back. "No, you mustn't. My face is evil."

"Impossible. Faces have not the power to be evil. Only the woman behind the face can be evil, and I do not believe that of you."

Looking down, Shelah was amazed to see the old man kissing the hem of his robe. "You are a true son of Shem, young Master. I have been telling my child this since the beard of Samuel only reached to his waist, but she has not listened to me." Benu'el turned to her. "Remove the veil!"

Perhaps the sound of his name stirred something in Samuel, for he renewed his bleating in a much louder voice, "Shoes, shoes, buy my father's shoes."

Even the old woman stirred and half-opened her lashless eyelids in time to see Tamar untie the black linen and slowly move it aside from her sun-abandoned face. Though she trembled so much that it took her fingers an eternity to do this simple task, and kept her dark eyes firmly cast to the ground, Tamar obeyed her father's command without further question.

Shelah could not help but catch his breath. Her beauty was far greater than he had imagined in spite of the stories he had heard. Time could only have touched such a face with the hand of an artist for she was now perfection embodied as far as he could see. High cheekbones, a small perfectly sloped nose and full lips accentuated her olive colored eyes. No wonder Onan had worshipped her beauty so much he had come to believe her Astarte. She wore no cosmetics at all, so the black eyes with their thick lashes, and the melon-pink lips gave the only color to the smooth pebble-white countenance. The gentle curve of her tiny chin made even him wish to calm its quiver. He could easily see why her beauty had entranced his father. He only wondered how he had resisted.

Judah stared into the face of the Egyptian Minister of Pharaoh. It somehow seemed to him a cruel face, though he knew women would find it appealing. Perhaps the Minister was enjoying their plight. Yet he was not willing to look at them as he pronounced his sentence. For three days, they had sat in the foul prison not knowing what was to be their fate. All because they had come to buy grain for their families. In a way, it might be funny; if he were in any mood to see humor. All the things he had done in his life, and now to be thrown in jail for trying to save lives.

Though he had to physically restrain his brother Levi, it seemed to Judah that the much harder task was to hold back his own fists as the palace guards led Simeon away. There were ten brothers here, and it would not be difficult to overpower the petty tyrant and his puny army. They had done worse than that before, though they were much younger then, of course, and had not been imprisoned for three days with scant food. But they would never make it out of the land of Egypt, and even if they did, without the promised grain, there would be too many at home who would die of starvation for their foolishness.

Spies, the young ruler had called them. How dare he? In times past, they had known wealth as great as ruler any here. They had dined with kings, and been presented gifts by the princes of many nations merely in hope of a blessing from the great God of the Habiri; Yah, Who brought forth water from the driest ground, and sent messengers with news of children born to barren women. Where was Yah now? Did He not care that His people were being humiliated before this pagan?

Pharaoh's Minister was dressed in scant, though rich, sheathing like the rest of the Egyptians. His bare chest and wrists were encased in jewel-encrusted gold. Yet he somehow had not the look of his countrymen. Perhaps it was only that his duties shielded him from the harshness of the sun's rays for most of his days. Duties? His hands were smooth and the nails clean and long. His skin showed no trace of manly hair, and glistened not with sweat, but with myrrh-scented oils. More than likely, someone else did all the work for him. Probably the pagan spent all his days in the arms of women; slave women, or more likely little boys who feared him as a god, a pretty god who had no need to fear anyone or anything.

Yet even this pagan claimed to fear Yah, did he not? His original plan had been to keep them all prisoner; to let only one of them go home with the grain on condition that he bring back Benjamin. What could he want with Ben? The boy was a bit simple-minded, and if Father weren't so wrapped up in Ben's resemblance to Joseph, he would see that. Even so, Benjamin was good-hearted, and he couldn't spend his life in an Egyptian prison, where every criminal in the land would make sport of him.

Judah attempted once more to approach the Minister of Pharaoh, and though he sought to master his harsh tone, it seemed unlikely to help his cause. "Listen, Sir, we are honest men, the sons of one father, as we have been trying to tell you. You have searched our bags, and seen that we carry much gold and silver, rubies and emeralds; certainly more than enough to buy the grain we need for our households. Why do you persist in believing us spies? Can you not see that we are not poor men; that we have no desire to take over your land?"

His eight brothers nodded, trying to lend weight to his words. Issachar and Naphtali even pulled out the little sacks of gold that still hung around their necks. They were rough men though. Nothing could hide that. The sun had baked their skin until it was almost as dark as an Ethiopian's was. And though their teeth were still as strong and milk-white as ever, cuts and scrapes had scarred all of them badly. Gad had broken his nose twice, and it was badly misshapen. Dan had a stump of a right foot from the encounter with Hamor. In addition, Asher was blind in his left eye from a fall over a cliff while rescuing a lamb from a briar thicket. Three days had not improved the stink in their rough traveling tunics either. Perhaps it was not so difficult after all to see why the Minister believed them spies.

As the interpreter whispered his words into the Minister's ear, the stony face did not change, though he pulled on his other ear as he listened. For a moment, Judah was reminded of another man. The interpreter spoke in a high-pitched monotone that had a vague resemblance to his own tongue.

"His majesty, the Pharaoh's Minister, says your question carries its own answer. Can a man eat gold and silver, or rubies and emeralds? This land has that which many have come from far away to buy or steal at any cost in this time of famine."

Accepting the truth of these words, Judah tried to appeal to any compassion the man might have, though his statue-like face revealed none. "Our Father is very old, Sir, and he has only one son left at home. Father loves him very much, as he reminds him much of another son whom he lost many years ago. If he loses this son, it may kill him."

Did he see sadness come over the Minister's face? Of course not. The guard had not even interpreted his words yet. Anyway, the face had turned away from him; did not look at him as the servant translated his answer.

The guard placed his palms together, and extended his arms as he bowed low before them. "His majesty, the Pharaoh's Minister, says to go home, and prove the truth of your words by returning with your brother. You may assure your Father that as the Pharaoh lives, if you do not speak falsely, your brother who stays and your brother who returns will come to no harm at his hands. So be it."

With these words, the interpreter bowed again and left the room, but though the Minister turned long enough to receive their bow to the floor with a nod, he did not actually leave. He backed into the shadows and appeared to be staring out a high window at the far side of the room. At least without his interpreter, the ruler could not understand the brother's words, for Reuben and Levi were at each other's throats with the same old argument. Judah and Issachar had to separate them before it came to actual blows.

Reuben recovered himself first. "Didn't I tell you not to sin against that boy? And you wouldn't listen. None of you would. Well, now comes the reckoning for his blood. Which one of you wants to be the one to tell Father about this? Anyone brave enough to do that? It doesn't take much courage for nine of you to tie up one boy and throw him in a pit, or to sell him bound and gagged to a wandering caravan headed to Egypt, does it? But, face Father and tell him he has to choose whether to lose one son or risk losing another too, and you're all faint-hearted." His angry voice softened. "I

Tokens of Promise

admit I am. In spite of his faults, I love the old man, and this really might kill him."

"Stop the foolish talk, Reuben. All of you. It doesn't do any good to blame each other now for a sin made over twenty years ago." Judah put his hand on Reuben's shoulder, and slowly Reuben nodded. "I'll tell Father. I don't like the task any more than you do, but I'm the one who came to him with a lie back then, and I can come to him with the truth now. Besides, I think I can break it to him more gently than any of you would."

As they all vigorously nodded their agreement, and began slapping each other on the back in an effort to appear in better spirits, Judah laughed. "Let's go home. These Egyptian houses stink. All I can smell is garlic."

Reuben looked around as if trying to locate the non-existent smell before he too joined his brothers in laughing. They went arm-in-arm out the wide palace door and almost ran to the stables. The palace guards had their donkeys saddled and waiting for them, and escorted them on their journey for almost the entire day that they might have no further time to plan any rescue attempt or raid.

It was not until nightfall, after the troop of guards had disappeared over the mountaintop, and they had stopped at a tiny inn to rest the animals and seek shelter from a threatening storm that Zebulon opened one of the feed sacks to make a fodder for his donkeys. "Judah, look here. The gold is still in my sack!"

"Yah, be merciful! No, it can't be." Judah went from donkey to donkey opening his own sacks. "Reuben, Issachar, Levi, come quickly. Check your sacks. The Egyptians have put our money back. Now what will we do? That wretched Minister will now put Simeon to death as a thief and a spy. He will never believe we did not steal his gold and his grain. I'm not sure I believe it, and I know it's the truth."

Nine blankets rolled out on the floor of the tiny inn that night, but not one of the brothers slept even for one watch. Fear that the troop of Egyptian guards would return with the pale-skinned Minister leading them was overpowered by a fear that it would not, and they would have to face Jacob with the loss of another son and a demand for a third.

❈ ❈ ❈

Tamar sat cross-legged on the floor between the chaises of Emi and her father while the young Master sat likewise between Father and Samuel. Emi had awakened for now, and was eager to hear the news from the young stranger. Although she referred to him once or twice as Judah, Tamar felt sure she knew who he really was, for she kept telling Tamar to get him a drink or some of her raisin cakes, and she would not have been nearly so friendly to his father. Emi blamed Judah for all the unhappiness in Tamar's life.

Tamar broke her silence. "Tell me, Young Master, is the Master's father, Jacob, still alive?"

A puzzled look crossed Shelah's face. "Yes, he is. Why do you ask?"

She shrugged, and clutched the gnarled fingers of her father. Her bitterness toward the reverent Man of God had evaporated long ago, leaving only a desire to please a gentle and loving father. "I'm not sure. I guess because your father seemed to love his father so much, but at the same time almost seemed to hate him. I wondered if they had resolved the conflict."

Shelah shook his head. "No, they are worse than ever. Is it not strange how the consequences of a problem can reach across so many generations to continue to plague a people?"

He stood up and gazed out at the courtyard while he wiped his sweaty palms on his tunic. "My father would not marry you because he would not have two wives. I cannot disagree with that. A man should only have one wife. But Father came to believe it not because of a revelation of Yah's truth, but only as a means to spite my grandfather; to prove to himself that he was a better man for his self-denial."

"And what of you, Young Master? Will you deny yourself any wife at all because of what your father has done?" She moved to look into his tanned but unlined face, but he avoided her eyes.

At last, sighing, he took her hands. "No, my dear sister, I won't. I intend to marry Ruah."

Chapter 4

Tamar covered her mouth with her palms, and kneaded her eyelids back and forth with the tips of her fingers as if she could somehow wipe away the pictures from the past that seemed to hover there. Finally, picking her words carefully, lest she offend the young Master, she said, "Are you certain that is wise, Sir? Ruah has had some problems in the past, and..."

"You needn't be afraid for my sake, my sister. Ruah has confessed to me her part in the tragedies. She was ill with grief, but she's better now, and she sends her deep desire for your pardon."

Ruah begged her pardon? The idea seemed somehow intensely funny, and Tamar fought to control the urge to laugh hysterically. The voice of the young Master spoke tenderly, and he sought to enfold her in the large prophet's mantle, but she withdrew from his and her father's penetrating gazes and went to sit silently alone under the giant palm tree in the courtyard. She had so much to think about as the past cast its shadows all around her.

Judah lifted his arms as he said his afternoon prayers, but the wish for a single withered twisted oak or palm tree to shade him from the fierce desert sun kept breaking his concentration. Finally, he gave up, sat on the small rock away from his brothers, poured a bit of water from his wineskin and rubbed his neck with it. In only three days, they would reach Hebron and he must pass the news to Jacob. Jacob would hate him for it; would blame him for not trying to find a way to save his brother, and would surely never send Benjamin to help them retrieve Simeon.

He looked at the caravan of donkeys gathered for their ration of water. That seemed like so much grain to look at, but how long would it feed them, even at strict portions? At least he had convinced his father that they had to free most of their slaves near the beginning of the famine, and most had gone safely back to their homelands or to their families. The thought of feeding nearly nine hundred people now made him shudder, where once it had seemed so trivial. Ashuah had always taken charge of the task of feeding his people so expertly he had never questioned how she did it.

How long before this grain ran out and they must go crawling back to that wretched Minister of Pharaoh or starve?

Perhaps the famine would end before then. Not likely. Even if it did, would that help them get Simeon back? How? Why did that pagan want Benjamin? Perhaps they could take a slave back. He couldn't possibly know the difference, could he? Somehow, even as the thought came to him, he shook it off. The man would know. He didn't know how, but he would. Maybe he was a seer. The Egyptians had many seers, and a man who rose to Pharaoh's Minister might especially be one. How else had Pharaoh known to put away so much grain? That was it. He must have told Pharaoh about the years of famine coming and this was how he was rewarded.

Did he also know of Joseph? Had he seen the sin of the brothers and decided to effect his own punishment? Why then would he want Benjamin? He was the only innocent brother. Thoughts whirled in his head.

"Judah," Reuben's voice seemed distant. "Judah, come on, wake up." Hard slaps struck both his cheeks. "You've been too long at your infernal prayers, my brother. The sun has stricken you. Drink."

Precious water was wasted as it trickled down his parched chin as Reuben's none-too-gentle fingers parted his cracked lips.

"You know better than to sit out here in this heat, Judah. Are you so desperate to get out of talking to Father?" His voice lowered almost to a whisper. "If so, I'll do it for you."

The whirling in his head slowed, and with Reuben's help, he stood up. "That's not necessary. Thank you for offering. I'm blessed to have you for my brother."

Waving away the compliment, Reuben led him down the hillside to the site they had picked out for their evening camp.

It was still a bit early, but the desert spread out before them as far as they could see, and they were not likely to find a better place before nightfall.

"Tamar, Tamar, come quick!" The panicky shout was heard long before anyone came into view. Shelah had assumed the town deserted except for Tamar and the three old ones. Evidently it was not so. In spite of the excited high pitch, the voice obviously belonged to a young man.

Tamar jumped up. "Joshua, we're in the courtyard," she called. "Come on through."

The face that appeared from the gloom was grinning widely, and the body that it belonged to wound itself around the sculptured pillar like a stem of a grape vine. "It's time! It's time! We need you, Tamar. You've got to come now!"

Shelah was surprised at the pangs of jealousy that assailed him as she went to the muscular young man in his short, sweat-stained tunic, and hugged him tightly.

"Are you sure this time, Josh? This is the third time you've come." At his emphatic nod, she patted his arm. "I'll get my things."

Shelah was about to protest when the old woman saved him from his foolishness. "Do you think you'll need my help, child? I may be old, but I can still deliver babies when I have to." Her bulging eyes seemed to smile and years dropped

Tokens of Promise 159

away from her at the prospect of bringing forth new life. "Is Sarai all right?"

Joshua shrugged and put his arm in Tamar's elbow to urge her to hurry.

"I think I can handle it, Emi. After all, I learned from the best teacher I know." She hesitated momentarily. "But why don't you come along anyway, just in case."

She said it lightly, as if to please the old woman, and no one else seemed to be bothered by the request, but something in the tone made Shelah wonder. He helped Emi rise from the chaise so molded to her figure. A jeweled cane lay under the couch, and he handed it to her even as her withered fingers reached for it. With surprising speed, the two women left.

Confusion and anxiety were apparent in his face as Joshua turned to follow them, but Benu'el called to him. "No, Josh, stay here. You must meet our guest."

As if seeing him for the first time, Joshua bowed. He wiped his dusty hands on the coarse tunic, and extended them in greeting. "I'm sorry for my lack of hospitality, friend. Don't I know you?"

"You had more important things on your mind, my friend. Is this your first child?" Joshua nodded. "I doubt you know me, but perhaps you have met my father." He reached to take the arm of the youth.

Joshua pulled away and unsheathed his knife. His fighting stance was threatening. "Of course. The Prince of Hebron. So, you've come at last. I thought something was strange. You even took off her veil. You couldn't wait. I swear before Yah, I'll not allow it. I'll kill you gladly before I'll let you hurt her again."

Backing up, Shelah raised his hands. The linen mantle slipped from one shoulder and he struggled to replace it while not coming too near Joshua's gleaming blade.

"Stop! I wouldn't hurt anyone, especially Tamar." His voice was even more squeaky than usual, and his fear shamed him.

"It's true, Josh." Benu'el confirmed. "He's a good man. See, I've given him my mantle. Now stop this foolishness."

Joshua lowered the knife, but continued to glare at Shelah. "But, Father Benu'el, he's going to take her away from us. What about what you always said about Yah's plan?"

The old man smiled. In spite of his age, he had a mouth full of white teeth, and his wide smile revealed all of them. "The plan will be," he said. "The boy has released her from her bond to him. He's going to help us make his father marry her instead."

"How?" Joshua demanded.

The three of them, not counting the present-in-body but absent-in-mind Samuel, sat in silence with their heads bowed, waiting for an idea of how to win the reluctant bridegroom.

"Joshua."

He looked up, a little guiltily, Shelah thought, to realize that he had forgotten entirely the purpose for his coming. Tamar stood framed in the archway, holding a small bundle wrapped in white linen.

"I almost didn't make it there in time. Your son was anxious to join us."

Joshua stared at the baby, transfixed by the tiny features.

"Wouldn't you like to hold him?"

As Joshua reached to take his son, he drew back his hands as Shelah shrieked, "That's it, that's it! As Yah lives, I think He has shown me His plan."

"What's it?" Joshua carefully took hold of his son, distracted from the conversation.

"You've found the answer. A babe. What man could give up his own son?"

Chapter 5

As Shelah explained his plan, Tamar stared at him in disbelief. How could he believe Yah would have such a plan? How could he believe she would do such a thing to a man she had loved for almost as long as she could remember? How could he even believe his father foolish enough to be tricked in such a manner? Or so desperate for a woman that he would even consider it? He could have any wife he chose, and now that Ashuah was dead, he wouldn't even be breaking his vow to Yah.

Six months now he had been alone, and men did get lonely. Somehow, she had hoped he would have forgiven her by now and come to her of his own accord. But he hadn't. She couldn't do this to him, she couldn't. Not that she could get away with it if she did. She rubbed her naked face with her hands. He hadn't seen her face in over twelve years now, but he would recognize it. Surely he would. Hadn't he once said that he could never forget it? Hadn't he also said that once he had planted a child in her belly, he would forget everything else in the world but her? Many men said such things and meant nothing by them, but not the Master. Surely not the Master.

Josh's voice broke into her thoughts. "Now, explain this plan to me one more time before I go back to Sarai. She'll want to know every detail."

Shelah nodded his head continuously as he recounted the plan. "Look, every year at the time of the full moon of next month, Father goes up to Timnath for the sheep shearing. Suppose you bring Tamar, dressed as a *zonah*, up to meet him at the crossroads of Enaim. I could even send Enos up to help you protect her. If you set up a tent there, you could both watch for him coming from the hillside behind it."

Tamar broke in. "It won't work, Young Master. Your father will recognize me immediately."

"But he hasn't seen your face in over..." Shelah started to protest. Then he shook his head. "No, you are right. What you must do then is to make up your face in the Canaanite fashion, you know, with that red around the eyes and green on your cheeks. Then you must return to a veil." He picked up the discarded black linen. "But not this wretched thing. Something as light as the mist on the mountain morning."

He stuffed the black veil in his girdle as if to assure himself she would not return to wearing it. "I will send the finest Hirah has to offer."

She sat on the foot of her father's chaise, and rested her chin on her tight fist. Her father lay back quietly staring at her. He offered no advice. She must work through every detail.

Again, she shook her head. "It is forbidden for a *zonah* to wear a veil in public, Shelah. If the Master has become as you say he has, he would stone me before he came anywhere near me."

He bit his thumbnail for a while in the manner so familiar in his father. Finally, he sighed. "Then there is no other choice. You must be a *qaseh*, a hierodule."

For a moment, she turned to stone. Then she screamed, "No!" and ran back into the shadows.

Even Benu'el looked shocked at this suggestion. If he had not still held the babe in his arms, Joshua would have surely struck Shelah. The oath Joshua swore at him was nearly as painful.

"No, wait, listen. I know my father. He would never treat you like...like...well, like that."

When she finally turned back toward him, there were still tears glistening in Tamar's eyes, but there was also anger. "There is no way he would ever come in to a temple whore at all." She wrung her hands. "Since it will be sheep shearing time, there will be no lack of customers ready to pray to their fertility gods by using me to toss their seed to the ground. But not your father. I know that much. Yah may be distant, but He is still the only God of Judah."

Shelah reached out to take her hand. "But that's just it, don't you see? The more you remind him that as a priestess, he must be sure not to get you pregnant, the more he will be certain to try to do just that. He would never waste his seed, but if you are alluring enough, he will take great pleasure in what he believes is thwarting the pagans by making their priestess pregnant with a son of Yah."

Benu'el laughed and nodded agreement. Soon Joshua and Shelah joined in, and their loud mirth awakened the baby and caused him to cry.

Joshua rose. "I'd best take him back to his mother and let Emi get some rest." He grasped Shelah's right arm. "Thanks, my brother. I will do whatever I can to help."

As the sun was setting, and the night breeze cooled the air, Tamar set about moving Samuel to his bed inside. Shelah followed her lead and helped Benu'el into the large inner room. As he began building the fire, and stirred the pottage Tamar brought to set on it, he thought aloud more of the details of his plan.

His father never carried money when he went to the sheep shearing. It was one of the few places he didn't. If Tamar were to ask for his belongings as payment until he could send her money, she would have proof of the identity of the man who had taken her. The tent would be dark, and she was not to stay outside long enough for him to get a close look at her.

Tamar listened as she worked. "But suppose he does come in to me, and recognizes me. It's one thing to deceive him at a distance, but quite another so close."

He shrugged. "Even if he does, what does it matter? Perhaps it would even be better. We just want him to recognize his own feelings, don't we? But he won't. Father will convince himself that any resemblance he sees is in his own mind." He took her hand. "My concern is more that he may hurt you. He won't be gentle because he will hate himself for his desire for you, and he will hate you for the evil practices he will think you represent. Are you sure he is worth it?"

It seemed so cruel. It was. She had always believed in honesty. Could the plan of Yah truly only be fulfilled by deception? It seemed the only way. Judah had called her his wife. She was his wife. It must be. It must. "Yes, I will do it. It is my destiny."

"I'm not sure I like this plan, child. It's too dangerous." Emi rolled the last strands of Tamar's black hair up into the pile of curls on her head and secured them with a bronze comb. She stood back to admire her work. Not that the child needed her help to look beautiful. The good God Yah had done a mighty work on that score already. "You'll do."

Intent on scraping her sharpened dagger across her thigh to remove every last hair from her body, Tamar might not have heard her. Finally, she looked up. "What do you mean? How dangerous? Both Joshua and Enos will be with me to protect me from any strangers. I wonder how I'm supposed to wear this." She held up the long strip of shiny gold cloth Shelah had sent to her and began to wrap it around her arms. "Isn't it funny? I've never even seen a real hierodule."

"Give me that, child, before you wrinkle it. Here, turn around, and let me do it."

Taking the length, she folded it in half and looped the center behind Tamar's neck. Carefully, she brought each piece down the sides of her breasts and cupped the bottoms to lift them up and together. Then she alternated winding each piece around the waist and down until they met again at the pubic mound with only a short length left hanging. She pinned a jeweled clasp to hold them in place. She stood back to check it.

"Now, hand me the veils." She eyed each piece critically as it was handed to her. "It's not strangers you need protecting from, child. Your man won't take kindly to being tricked. He might even deny ever having been near you, or suppose he claims there were others. You've had two husbands, so it's not as if you had your blood to prove it to him. He could have you stoned, or your father being who he is, he could have you burned alive."

The child's eyes became enlarged and glazed as they had so often done in the past when she had one of her visions. Emi wiped the sweat from her forehead. "I'm sorry, child. I didn't mean to upset you so. He won't do that to you. He won't. I won't let him. And your father won't." She lifted the wineskin to the child's lips and tilted her head back, pouring as much of the burning liquid down her throat as she could without spilling too much of it on the exotic cloth. Tamar was coming out of it. She began to cough. Emi wasn't sure; her hearing wasn't what it used to be, but surely she said, "Two husbands...blood...more blood...still more blood...will there ever be enough?"

Tokens of Promise

Emi kept pouring more wine into Tamar despite her protests that she was perfectly fine now. She did feel better; lightheaded even. She spun around and admired the layers and layers of veils with their jeweled clasps that gleamed in the lamp light, and tried to listen as Emi explained how to attach them. She would have to learn to dress herself like this before she went to Enaim in just a few days. Emi was right about the Master. She would have to get a token from him so that there was no way that he could deny that it was his child; better yet, more than one token. She must decide what she should ask for.

She looked down at her veiled body. Her belly was still as flat as it had been as a girl, but her breasts, hips and buttocks had filled out a bit. That would probably please the Master, she decided. She would look better when she wore her powders and cosmetics, but somehow already she felt young again.

She danced outside. Joshua sat on a chaise quietly talking to her father. Swaying up to him, she took his hand and demanded, "What do you think, Josh? How am I?" She lowered her voice to a husky whisper and trailed the veils down his arm. "Could I seduce you? Does just looking at me make you want to take me to bed?"

His fierce reaction sobered her when he drew back his hand as if scalded. The swift intake of his breath and his scarlet face shamed her. "Please don't do that to me, Tamar. I am a man, and Sarai's time is not yet up. It's cruel to tempt me so."

She was stunned. He was her brother-in-law; had always been like her little brother. Were all men so possessed by their bodies? She ran back into the house.

Benu'el stared at him. "Does Sarai know?"

"Of course." Joshua couldn't keep the bitterness out of his voice. "It isn't the kind of thing I could hide from her if I wanted to. But she's always known. It's our curse."

Joshua looked his father-in-law in the eye. "I would have taken Tamar years ago if you had allowed it. You've known that."

"Yes, but I thought you'd gotten over it. I thought you were happy with Sarai."

"I am. I love her too, in a way. She's gentler than Tamar, and she loves her sister even more than I do. She's not as beautiful, but..."

He jumped up suddenly. "Look, why don't we just give up this wild scheme. I'll marry both of them, and we can be a happy family together. I'd take care of them. I promise."

"No." Benu'el remained calm. "As you stand outside that tent in a few days, you will burn because another man is inside taking Tamar. Then you will understand what you would do to my Sarai if I allowed you to take her sister. I will not allow it."

He slumped back and buried his head in his rough hands. "You're right. It would never work. I'll do all you ask."

Chapter 6

"I see him, Mistress," Enos called. "He's just coming over the rise. He should arrive with the evening breeze."

"Thank you, Enos. I will be ready." Tamar breathed deeply. Enos and Joshua had prepared her tent and were waiting on the hillside behind it. She had no worry that the Master would recognize them, dressed as they were in the flowing robes of attendants to a Canaanite priestess. Wine and mandrakes had taken away most of her fear. All that remained was restlessness, and a desire to have done with the whole affair as soon as possible.

She surveyed the tent. It was very different from the tents of the Habiri; the material being an almost crimson shade, and the cushions soft and inviting in the pale glow of the scented oil lamps that sat on mats all around the edge. It seemed that Shelah had thought of everything; she wondered how he knew.

She combed out her hair once again with the bronze combs and piled curls at the crown as Emi had taught her. She washed her body once again in goat milk and applied the soothing myrrh ointment. The veils were wisps that she could blow away with a light breath, like the pollen from a spring flower, but by the time she had put on the many layers that Shelah had sent, her own vision was clouded and she knew the Master could not see her face clearly. Gold chains and jewels shimmered beneath the veils they held in place. She had bread, cheese, and wine ready for the Master, as well as cool water to bathe him in if he desired. It would be hard not to slip and call him Master, but even if she did, he would probably think nothing of it. Her voice had deepened over the years, hadn't it? Nevertheless, it would be better to say as little as possible. What should she call him then? She sat back on the cushion and contemplated. "Yah, in Your wisdom, if this is truly Your will, smile on me and put words in my lips that it may be so."

As he neared Enaim, Judah became more and more agitated. There had never before been a hierodule's tent at the crossroads. Those foul Canaanites would do anything in honor of the evil Baalim. How dare they? Their wicked ways must be punished. Why didn't Yah smite them where they stood and show them that Yah was the Almighty? The fools. A man's seed was meant to bring forth men, not corn, or lentils, or sheep. It was abominable that the woman was allowed to practice her witchery on fools.

Then she came out. Yah, he must be bewitched. She was so beautiful. A man who was hungry and thirsting to the point of death could not realize it for the need to look upon her. He cursed himself for his own weakness. The creature was evil. Why would Yah make such a vision of her? How could such great evil be enshrined in such loveliness? Glints of gold dazzled his eyes, and the pale veils floating with the evening breeze enticed him, and made him ache. He drew closer.

"Good evening, Weary Traveler," she said in a voice barely above a whisper.

"What are you doing here?" he demanded as harshly as he was able.

"That should be obvious to one as good as you, my friend." Her hips wiggled sensuously in emphasis.

He cast his eyes to the ground. Better not to look on such wickedness. "Yes, well...you've never been here before."

He was stammering like a child. He glanced up, and then lowered his eyes as she beckoned him with her dainty jeweled hand.

"What did you say, Sir? I could not hear you." She stepped closer, and the scent of her filled his nostrils with delight.

"Um...I said...I wonder if you might have a drink of cool water? Mine has become hot."

She smiled and held back the flap of the inviting tent. "Of course, Sir. Come inside and rest while I draw it for you."

Hesitating only a moment, Judah stepped into the dimly lit oasis. It was wine she handed him, not water, but that did not really surprise him. There was food set out on a mat as if she were expecting him. That was impossible, but perhaps she kept food prepared. With her obvious beauty, she would have no lack of men coming to her. She moved with a slight hesitation as if new to this, but it was probably only his imagination. She rubbed his shoulders to soothe away the weariness expertly enough. He ate, and his eyes feasted on her. He tried to pull her to him.

She leaned away. "First you must buy my favor, Sir. What will you pay?"

"I'll give you ten silver shekels."

"Gold."

"Done, but I'll have to send it back to you. I'm going up to shear my sheep, and I never carry that much money with me to the fields. There are too many thieves about."

She laughed her trilling laugh, and came closer again. Her perfume entranced him.

"And how may I know that you are not one of them?"

"Don't be foolish, woman. Anyone could tell you who I am. You will get your money."

She shook her head. "That will take too long. I may not still be here then. The time of the shearing is almost past, and I have a better place in mind. I know. I will take a firstling of your kids. That won't take as long, and I could do well with some goat milk."

"The firstling is sacred to Yah. I'd rather send the money."

"No. I'll have the kid. It may be redeemed according to your law."

He grabbed for her, but she eluded him, leaving him holding a wisp of veil from her right thigh. "You know much for a Canaanite woman. You will get your kid."

She laughed and plucked the veil from his fingers. "Of course I will. And until I do, you will leave me tokens of your identity, that you may not accuse me of being a liar and a thief."

He was becoming angry but also weary. "What do you want?"

"Your staff."

"Take it."

"And your ring." She trailed the veil across his face. His nostrils filled with its delicate fragrance.

Shrugging, he pulled it off. "Here, have it if you wish. It is worth far more than your price, but I will pay it."

"And your mantle."

"No, you will not. The shawl of Yah cannot be given to a pagan." *How dare she?*

"I will have it."

He shook his head. "You don't need it. The ring has my mark. It is known throughout the area as my seal. Anyone will tell you who it belongs to."

The veils shook. "No, I will also have the mantle."

She dropped a veil into his lap. Nervously, Judah fingered the long tassels at the corners of his shawl and pulled it close to his shoulders.

"Why do you want it? It's only a prayer shawl. It's old and worn and not at all valuable. What could you possibly do with it?"

"You value it, as you do not the ring and the staff. So...you will not forget me." She began removing the veils as she walked around extinguishing the dim lamps. Her body swayed gently as she walked. "Will you pay?"

As the last lamp went out behind him, her slim fingers lifted the mantle from his shoulders.

"You know I will," he muttered, as she fell into his arms. He meant to say, "Yah forgive me," but it was smothered in her kisses.

The Master was asleep. She suspected there was something in the wine Emi gave her for him, but possibly he was only exhausted from his long walk. Hurriedly, she dressed herself in her traveling garment and threw the tokens out to Joshua. She must be far away by the time he awakened. She hugged her body. It felt strange to her. Shelah had been right about his father, and yet wrong too. He was angry and not gentle at first, yet he had given her pleasure.

She didn't think he had guessed she was not what she pretended. It had been much easier than she had expected to respond to his touch, and even to touch back. At the last moment, she had remembered to warn him that he must not make her pregnant. He had laughed and immediately filled her with his seed. Of course. Just as Shelah had said he would. She cradled her flat belly as if she could already feel the baby growing inside of her. The Master's baby. Her baby. The fruit of their love. Gazing one last time at the sleeping face, so gentle in rest, suddenly she felt sad. She loved him, longed to lie beside him and feel his arms enfold her, reach for her, and come in to her.

She shook herself free from the lethargy that threatened to overcome her. *He does not love me. He only made a business deal with a whore to soothe the pain in his groin for a time.* He hadn't even pretended anything else. She wondered why she had thought he might recognize her. Obviously, her image was gone from his memory.

Judah jerked awake; her name on his lips as always. Where was he? Why did his head ache so? Oh...yes...He looked around. The red tent of the hierodule. Where was she? He stumbled to the tent flap to stare out at the predawn gloom. He licked his lips. No sign of the priestess or of her slaves. Rubbing his neck, he backed inside. He lit each of the lamps in turn, searching the area around it. Though the cushions still held the seductive scent of her, there was no other sign that she had ever been there. No combs, no clothing, no hair, nothing. She had even taken the blanket they had lain on. Only a plate of cheese and figs lay prepared for him by the door, but he was not hungry. His mantle, ring and staff were missing, but that was expected. Lying back on the cushions, he closed his eyes.

She was again in his arms; her flesh molded to his. Feeling puzzled by her seeming inexperience, and yet pleased by it, he chided himself for a fool. Most likely, she wasn't innocent at all. It was an act that excited her gullible customers. *Adept enough at her bargaining, wasn't she?*

He'd best get his things back as quickly as possible. He'd send Hirah back with the kid. The temptation in meeting her again himself was too great by far, though it pained him to admit his own weakness. Why did Yah put such a fire in a man? Ah well, Hirah would take pleasure in looking on her, even if he was too old now to lie with her. He was too old, wasn't he? He shook his head at his own folly.

A whore. A filthy pagan whore. Why then was she so blessedly beautiful?

Chapter 7

Shelah ran up the hillside. Sliding down to lie beside the weeping figure, he put his hand on her trembling shoulder, but she shook it away. "Ruah, what's wrong? Why are you crying?"

She turned to him, her face stained with tears and dirt. "I thought you were different from your brothers, but you couldn't resist her, could you? I thought you really cared for me." She turned her face back to the ground.

"I do care for you, woman." He sat up and tossed a pebble. "I have given you no reason to doubt me."

Ruah wiped her eyes; the dirt smeared across her cheek. "You went to see her. You even told me you did." She sniffed. "But you said you released her from her bond to you."

He put his arm back on her shoulder. This time she didn't thrust it away. "So...I did. I didn't lie to you, Ruah."

"You did. You gave her a baby so your father would have to consent to the wedding." She hid her face in her sleeve. "You're just like Er. You couldn't look upon her without taking her."

Shelah waited until her sobbing had slowed. "How do you know Tamar is with child?" He gently turned her to face him and held her quivering chin.

"The servant you sent with the new supply of food told me."

"What did he say exactly?"

"That every morning she wretches at the sight of food, and that he was to tell you alone that it has been three moons since the way of women has come upon her."

"Then why did he tell you instead of me? I will have him whipped for his loose tongue." He stood up and looked out at the horizon. "Who else do you think he told?"

"No one, I swear." He could hardly hear her whisper. "So it is true. Her beauty won you."

More calmly, he sat back down. "Yes, her beauty won me, but not the way you believe, my love. I greeted her and left her as my sister. I am not the one who made her with child."

"Then why did she insist that no one but you be told the news? Do you know who the father is?"

"Yes."

"Well, tell me, Shelah."

"I cannot."

"Why?"

"You will tell my father."

"So? He should be told she has played the harlot. Everyone has always seen her as so, so holy. Shouldn't they now see her for what she is?" Her anger made her voice grow shriller.

Shelah's eyes widened. "Perhaps you are right. You must tell my father. Do one thing though. Use those exact words. Say, 'Tamar has played the harlot, and she is with child.' Promise me you will use those exact words."

Ruah stared at his too innocent face. "What are you plotting, Shelah? I want to know, or I won't tell him."

He shrugged. "All right, don't tell him. It was your idea."

"You're playing with me, Shelah. What is it you would really have me to do?"

"Tell him."

"Why?"

"I can't tell you."

"What if I won't?"

"Then you prove to me that your hatred of Tamar is stronger than your love for me." Shelah stood with his back turned to her.

Ruah caught her breath. "Are you saying you won't marry me if I do not tell?"

"Yes."

He walked away.

Hirah paced the tent. "I want to know what you have been plotting, boy. First you send Oni to me with a request for lengths of the finest gold cloth I have and enough red material to make clothing for fifty women, gold and jewels fit to adorn a bride."

He stopped pacing and stared at Shelah. When no explanation was forthcoming, he resumed pacing. "I thought you finally made your father see reason, and were going to Chezib to claim your bride. But I hear no such news."

Picking up the wine vat with one hand, Hirah poured himself a bowl and emptied it with one swallow. He poured another. "Then your father tells me this strange story of a nonexistent harlot he describes as dressed all in fine gold veiling, and dwelling at the crossroads at Enaim in a red tent. I went all over that town trying to deliver a goat to a woman no one had ever heard of before. Then I remembered you and your cloths. Do you think me a fool, Shelah, that I don't know this is your doing? Do you deny it?"

He drained the bowl again, and set the wine vat back in place.

Shelah looked up. Hirah's face was full of fury. "No."

Hirah wiped his mouth with his forearm. "But why? Only your God Yah could see reason in such strangeness."

"The reason is simple, my good friend Hirah. My father's eyes needed to be opened." Shelah stood and wrapped himself tightly in Benu'el's mantle.

"And are they?"

"Not yet. But soon."

"And you want me not to tell him of our transactions?" Hirah faced the black tent wall. "I've never lied to your father, Shelah. There has always been trust between us."

"Trust me, Hirah. I love my father, and I did not do this to harm him." Shelah kept silent as the big man paced back and forth in the dim tent.

"As I live, son, if you have deceived me to no purpose, you'll sleep with Yah for the rest of your days. For now I will abide by your will." Without another word, he turned and left the tent.

"So that is the way of it."
"You were listening?"
"Yes."
Reaching out, he drew her into the tent, and looked out to see that no one else was near. "Ruah, when will you learn not to listen to what is not meant for your ears?"

"Never." She folded her arms across each other.

"You speak truly, woman. Why must you know what you shouldn't?"

She shrugged. "Perhaps I have often found the need to know that which men felt I shouldn't."

"But this has nothing to do with you."

"Somehow everything to do with Tamar has to do with me." She sat down. "Tell me everything."

"If you heard the entire conversation, you probably already know." He hoped that perhaps she had only caught the end, which told her nothing, and was trying to make him reveal the rest of the trickery.

"Tamar was the harlot your father met at Enaim, true?"

He groaned. "Yes."

Ruah clasped her knees and buried her face in them. "Forgive me, my love, for ever doubting you. You didn't lie to me."

Shelah pulled her to her feet. "I told you I had never lied to you. Now will you do my bidding?"

She nodded. "Will you marry me?"

"Yes." They kissed. Ruah sighed contentedly. "Would you truly have refused to marry me if I did not tell?"

"Do you want me to answer that?" His lips met hers again.

She laughed. "No. Never."

Chapter 8

Ruah came running to their meeting place, her hair blowing behind her in the evening breeze. Her cheeks were stained, and her eyes wet with tears. She fell, heaving for breath, at Shelah's knees.

"I have never seen him so furious, my love. I thought not to escape with my life."

"Truly, or do you exaggerate?" Though her face told of her fright, he wanted to know just how deeply his father was affected.

"He struck me, Shelah. He's never done that, not even when I told him what Er did. He said I was a lying whore who wasn't fit to wash the feet of one as pure as Tamar."

Shelah sat down. Absently he stroked her hair. "Don't cry anymore. It's over."

She laid her head in his lap like a little child. For a long while, they were both completely silent.

Finally, Shelah had to ask more questions. "Did he believe you, do you think?"

She nodded. "He didn't want to, but he called for the messenger, and he told the Master just what you told him to."

A new thought caused him to gasp. "Does Father know I went to Chezib?"

And as often happened between them, she read the direction of his thoughts. "Yes, but he knows it was too long ago. She would be heavy with child by now if you were the father." She giggled. "I don't know why I didn't realize that myself."

He kissed her forehead. "Jealousy blinds us."

He stood up and began to pace. "But doesn't he wonder why I went there?"

"That doesn't seem to have occurred to him yet." Ruah took his hand and he lifted her up. "But it will soon. And then what will you tell him?"

Shelah shrugged. "Maybe that I was curious to see my bride who was so beautiful she made grown men act like fools."

"That's a lie."

"So?"

"Nothing. I've just never known you to lie before." She turned away.

Gently, Shelah took her shoulder and turned her back to him. "And you won't now. I'll tell him the truth. I went to Chezib to release Tamar from her bond to me so that I could marry you."

"You would truly tell your father that?" Her eyes glistened with tears.

"Yes. It's time he learned to look on you as his daughter. And if he ever strikes you again, he will do battle with another son, and I doubt he will be the victor this time. Let's go."

"Where?"

"To Father. We've got to plan a wedding, and there isn't much time."

"Not much time, why ever not?"

"The barley feast is only a few weeks away, and I want to be married then."

"Why?"

"Why not? Won't you have me after all?" He began to race down the hillside, and Ruah ran laughing behind him.

Shelah sat cross-legged in his father's tent and stared at him across the fire. "But Father, I have told you...I released Tamar from her bond to me. You have no right to accuse her of anything. She was free to seek any husband she chose. Why must you persist in this fury?"

Speechless, Judah sat glaring at him. "You may have released her as you say now, perhaps in your compassion to save her life, but I did not, and I am still the head of this family. If she had wanted release, she should have come to me." He softened his bark somewhat. "Look son, you're still a bare-chinned youth, so innocent of the ways of the world, and the cunning of women. You..."

Shelah broke in. "No. She did not trick me, Father. I went there for the purpose of releasing her. Ruah is my chosen bride, and I will have no other. Together we will raise many sons to Yah." Shelah stood to leave.

"But Tamar..."

"...Is my sister. No more. Ruah pleases me as much as a man need be, and now Tamar belongs to another, so the matter is settled. Leave her in peace!"

"No! She has played the harlot, and she will be punished!"

Shelah turned back toward his father. He kept his head bowed but rubbed the toe of his sandal back and forth across the matted black goat hair mat. He whispered, "And will you then cast the first stone at her, Father?"

Judah stood and crossed his arms across his chest. He stared at his son. "I will not have to. Old Benu'el is a Son of Shem. She will not be stoned. She will be burned."

Chapter 9

Emi sat watching Tamar in her fitful sleep. Emi didn't seem to sleep so much these days. She kept vigil. Maybe the good God Yah had let her rest so much all those years to make up for all the sleep she was missing out on nowadays. Praise Yah it couldn't go on much longer. The poor child was already so great, she looked fit to bust. No way was she going to carry those babes through another two moons. Not with all she'd been through already. What with that fool man dragging her out of her home and down here to face his fancy family council. And the rumors flying all over the camp that he was going to burn her as a demon child, a priestess turned to *HaSatan*. No wonder she was so terrified, and cried out so often in her sleep. And the worst was yet to come, thanks to that man. He called himself master. Master of what, she wanted to know. He couldn't even master himself, much less... The poor child was moaning again. Give him his lot. He must be worth something the way she cared for him. She'd die for him. Probably was going to.

Emi soothed Tamar's sweaty brow with a damp cloth. "Hush, child. Emi's here, and she won't let a man hurt her babe." She continued her soft rhythmic chant until she too was nearly asleep. A sudden jerk reawakened her.

Tamar sat up, doubled over and breathing hard. "Oh, Emi, it hurts so. Is it time, do you think?"

"Not yet. They been beating up on you something fierce tonight though, haven't they?" She dipped the cloth in a bowl of sweet wine, and pressed it to Tamar's lips.

Tamar smiled weakly. "They must be taking out their father's anger on me." She clutched her bulging belly. "And he must be madder than a trapped viper. Are you sure at least one of them is a son, Emi?"

"If it isn't, may I give up my birthing stool forever. Do you think two female babes would be so blessed anxious to get out into this wicked world? As Yah lives, they'd have to be fools, and no babe of yours could be that, even if it did belong to that wicked man." She pulled the goat-hair sleeping rug up around Tamar's chin. "Why do you ask such a question? Are you afraid he won't accept claim if they're born girl babes instead of sons?" Emi shook her head sadly. "It's true some men mightn't. They say all a girl babe is good for is to bring his gold to another man's tent."

Tamar arched her back and loosened her hair from sticking to it. "No, it's not that. I don't think. He's not like that." She bit her lip and pulled the blanket back up. "At least he never used to be."

"But you're not sure. He's changed. Even you admit that."

Tamar nodded, unable to speak because of another spasm. Emi handed her the cloth to bite on. As it passed, Tamar lay back to rest.

"He has changed. The man who rescued me from Ben Qara is buried in a tomb of bitterness. I'm sure he's still alive in there somewhere, and I've somehow got to reach him."

Emi grunted. "How? He's putting you on trial for your life tomorrow before that infernal family council of his. How are you going to convince them not to burn you when you won't tell them he's the father?"

Tamar was staring into the flame of the clay lamp by the tent flap. "I had a dream last night, Emi. I dreamed the Master was reaching out to me, but as I tried to step closer and closer to him, he kept getting farther and farther away. Finally, I could barely see him anymore. There was a wall of light between us, but where he was, it was totally dark. Only his face remained in the blur of light."

Emi sat quietly, not daring to speak lest the child was having one of her visions again.

"Emi, wake up. Please, I need to talk with you."

"I wasn't asleep, child. I was just resting these weary eyes."

Tamar smothered her laugh, and Emi laughed too. Old Benu'el was fond of saying that when Emi rested her eyes, the dead couldn't rest.

"Emi, I had a dream last night."

"I heard you. You tried to get to your man, but you couldn't 'cause you were separated by a wall of flames."

Tamar gasped. "I didn't say that. How did you know?"

"It don't take a seer to know you're terrified by what he's planning to do to you tomorrow. Why don't you go to him tonight, before his family council, and tell him the truth. Show him the tokens, and get this thing over with. Why must you wait?" She shook her bony finger. "It's not good for the babes!"

Tama looked almost convinced, but she finally shook her head. "Father forbids it. He says the time is not yet ripe."

"The time is rotting!" Emi snorted. "Benu'el's an old goat, if I do say it! If he'd have stood firm in the first place, none of this would've happened. When does he think the time will be ripe, that's what I want to know; when the flames are licking the babe's milk from your breasts?"

Tamar gasped and covered her eyes. "Stop, Emi! You're frightening me."

"Maybe you needed frightening a bit, so you'd put an end to this." She stood to go. "I'll get you the tokens. You…"

Tamar clutched her arm. "I can't, Emi. I wish I could, but I can't. Not until Father says I can."

Defeated, Emi sat back down. Neither spoke for a long while, but neither slept. Finally, Tamar began reciting another dream, one she said she had had many times.

"I was ready to tell Judah the truth. Father had given his permission, and I was so happy because at last everything was going to be fine. I went to the hiding place behind the wine pots to get the tokens, but they were gone. I pulled aside every rug and blanket, and I ran back and forth between you and Shelah and Father to ask where you had moved them, but none of you knew anything about them. I asked the slaves if they had taken anything, but they denied it, and I wanted to beat them, but I knew they were telling the truth. They didn't take them. Then he appeared: *Samael*, the evil angel of

HaSatan, laughing at me for my fear. He laughed and laughed. He held them out to me, and I tried to grab them, but they scalded my hands. Then he slithered up close to me, until I could feel his breath on my neck, and I shivered with cold. He whispered to me that I could have them back easily if I would lie with him. He said that I had played the harlot with the Master, so why not with him? Then he laughed again, and as he put his cold hand on my belly, and promised not to touch the babes, his face changed into Er's, and that evil smile was wide just like it was before. I screamed again and again, but no sound came out, and no one heard."

"No man nor angel is going to steal them things, child. Not while I'm around. I'll get them right now and put them under my pillow."

Again, Tamar held her back. "No, Emi. Don't touch them. Leave them where they are. If I am truly to be the Master's wife, Yah will protect them better than you or I ever could. Isn't it strange? Er's face frightened me much more than Samael's. His laughter was so evil. So many times I've remembered that face and wished Yah had taken me that night instead of him."

Emi grunted. "And how about them babes inside you? Did you wish them not to be born?"

She gasped. "No, of course not. They're his. They're mine. How could I wish such a thing?"

"Well, if you're wishing you'd died back then, that's exactly what you are wishing. Now I don't want to hear any more such foolish talk. Lie back and get some sleep. I got to get a little rest for these weary bones." She closed her eyes and pretended sleep until the startled Tamar finally did as she was told.

Chapter 10

The hillside was covered with a mass of people, much as it had been on the day she had married Er. People had spread blankets everywhere, and there were a few baskets of food scattered about, but the mood was decidedly not festive. Children were fighting over crumbs, and their parents yelled harshly at them, and at each other. A few hurled insults at her, but many were too involved in their own quarrels. Food was jealously guarded, but slyly snatched at every distraction. A few stones pelted the tent when she peeped through the tiny opening. She jumped back just in time to dodge one aimed at her eye.

"Get back in here, child. No need to give them their blood before they demand it." Emi's gentle hands betrayed the harshness of her words, and Tamar gladly followed her to the cushion.

"Why do they hate me so, Emi? I knew the Master was angry, but what have I done to them?"

Emi snickered. "Nothing. Didn't have to. People got real trouble nowadays. Won't rain. Ground's so hard you can't get a stick in it to even begin to plant a crop. More animals dying every day. Even the babes are dying. Yah's angry, and they need someone to blame." She shrugged. "You're it. If a priest's daughter turned evil, it might be enough to offend Yah. They kill her, it might satisfy Him. He might make it rain. That's a good enough reason."

Tamar's mouth dropped open. Such reasoning had never occurred to her. "You don't really believe I'm to blame for the drought, do you, Emi?"

"Course not. I'm just telling you what they're saying. If they blame you, it's easier on them. They don't have to look inside themselves." She shoved a bowl of lentils at Tamar. "Here, eat something. You got to feed those babes."

Tamar nodded, and absently took the wooden bowl and stirred the warm lentils. She was surprised by a voice at her back as Ruah crawled under the tent cloth. Foolish town dweller that she was, it had never occurred to Tamar that Onan didn't need an opening in the tent. He'd just lain on his belly and scooted under. She laughed. A mystery solved after all these years. It was so simple. Ruah and Emi looked baffled by her laughter, and Ruah was about to back out.

"May I come in?"

Tamar stifled her giggles and motioned her in. "Quickly, before someone sees you. Don't be upset by my laugh, I was just remembering something, and I'm amazed at my own ignorance."

Ruah stared at her.

"You shouldn't have come here today." Tamar set the lentil bowl aside. "You might have been hurt."

Wiping dirt from eyes, and at the same time streaking her face, Ruah stood tall. "I should have come before, but I was afraid."

"I don't blame you. That's an angry mob out there. Go back to Shelah. He will protect you."

Ruah shook her head. "I'm not afraid of the mob. It's you I feared."

"Me? Why?"

Falling on her knees, Ruah bowed before her. "Because of all I did to you. I'm the one who convinced Onan you were Astarte. I didn't mean for what he did to happen. I liked Onan." She bit her lip. "I wanted him to kill you for what happened to Er. I never thought he would...would..."

Tamar rubbed Ruah's head and comforted her like a babe. "Hush now. You were ill back then, and it's all in the past. Shelah tells me you've changed, and now I believe him."

Ruah nodded.

"You're forgiven then. Go before you get caught in this."

Ruah shook her head. "No, I will serve you. Shelah would have you to look your finest before the council."

Emi nodded agreement and pushed the bowl of lentils back at Tamar.

"It would be dangerous to stay here. I'll tell Shelah I made you leave. You needn't fear."

Laughing, Ruah set to readying the washing ointments. "I don't fear. I serve gladly."

"See, I told you she'd changed." Shelah's head peeped through the same place Ruah had entered.

Ruah flicked the end of his nose with the towel. "Now who's listening where they have no business?"

Judah stared at his brothers. This was the first he had seen of them since their return from Egypt, and somehow they seemed incomplete without Simeon. Ben kept trying to join them and run about with a couple of the nephews who were about his age, but Father kept calling him back to his side as if one of them might use this as an excuse to steal the boy and cart him off to Egypt. The same anger that had tormented him for years welled up in him with a mighty strength.

He stood supervising the building of a large bonfire. It was the heart of the winter, and by this time, days of rain should have left a damp chill in the air. Instead, there had been no end to the sweat on his neck and the caked dust in his throat. The dry wood burned up too quickly, catching as the lighted lupine grass bundles were touched to it. He stared into the flame, hardly aware of Shelah hopping around him, trying to get his attention.

"Put a stop to this, Father. I keep telling you she's not guilty of anything." His words were barely discernible for his nibbling on his thumb.

"How can you continue to say that? Her belly proves her guilt."

"Of what? I've told you again and again that I released her. Why won't you listen?" Shelah pulled at his robe as he had done as a tot, but Judah continued to stare into the fire.

"Infidelity. She's an unfaithful harlot."

"Unfaithful to whom? To whom was she unfaithful? Can't you hear me? I keep telling you I released her."

Judah shook his head and picked up a large stick to throw on the fire.

Father Jacob's robe was of finely embroidered scarlet linen more appropriate to the Court of Pharaoh than to a desert tent camp. In fact, he might have been a king, such was his manner as he commanded slaves to place his mountain of cushions and blankets and bring him baskets of figs and a larger wine pot of better wine.

He seemed older, in some ways, than Grandfather Isaac who was so old that he was almost completely blind and deaf now, and his white hair had turned the color of melted gold. Yet Isaac's eyes wrinkled with laughter as his great-grandsons vied for the privilege of sitting on his lap and hugging him or running their fingers through his soft beard. His linen festal robe was soiled as grubby fingers held on to it and pressed close to him. Each child was lifted off with a pat on his bottom and a gold shekel in his greedy fingers.

As the sun came to stand directly overhead, Judah raised his arms. "Bring her forth."

His voice boomed across the mountain. All those who heard it ceased their bickering and assembled themselves as near to the family as they could get. A hush fell over the hillside. Even the children were pulled to their mothers' knees and quieted.

Two servants proceeded up the hill toward her tent. As they approached it, Emi and Ruah stepped out and lifted the tent flap aside. Tamar came out and looked over the crowd. Her white linen tunic was bright against the black goat hair, and her own black hair streamed over pale arms.

She still looked like a priestess or a bride in spite of her protuberant belly, and she had not attempted to hide her condition at all. Rather she had strands of jewels crossing between her breasts accentuating the roundness beneath. She held her head high as the two slaves stood aside to let her pass. They had no need of their blades as they, followed by Emi and Ruah, fell into step behind her.

Judah gazed at the ground to keep his traitorous eyes from being bewitched as the procession came nearer. Her hair brushed his arm as she stepped into the circle.

Someone threw a rock.

"Stop! The law is not yet fulfilled. She must first face the judgment of the council. Then you may do as you will with her!"

Though she had not flinched at the rock, her eyes looked at his as if he had been the one who had struck her. He turned away.

"Let it begin!" a voice shouted. Others joined a chorus of assent.

He cleared his throat. No words came.

Father Jacob stepped forward. "Yes, let it. Judah what is your charge against this woman?"

Jacob laid himself in his cushions as if they were a throne, and he the Ruler of Creation.

Judah turned back to Tamar and fixed his gaze on her belly. "She is an adulteress. She has played the harlot."

"Was she taken in adultery?" Jacob asked, grabbing a fig.

Glancing at his father, Judah shook his head. "No, of course not. It wasn't discovered until...look at her...It's obvious, isn't it?"

"But suppose she was not taken in adultery? How do we know? Perhaps her husband has given her this child."

Now Judah glared at Jacob. "No. Shelah has not taken her. It is not his child."

"How can you be so sure? Perhaps we should talk to the boy." Plunging the last of the fig into his mouth, he licked his fingers and reached for another.

Judah stayed his hand. "No! He's a child, and he has no place here. I'm his father, and I say it's not his babe. That should be enough for this council."

Wrenching free his hand and taking the fruit, Jacob stood facing him. "And I say it's not. If you want a judgment from me, I will hear from him."

"Gladly," Shelah shouted, breaking through the crowd. "I am not a child. I'm two years past the age I could appear before the council, and by the way, two years past the age I could be given a wife."

Coming to a halt between his father and grandfather, Shelah glared at them both fiercely.

Isaac broke the tense silence by directing Carmi, one of Reuben's sons, to repeat to him what was going on. While Carmi complied, everyone waited. Finally, in his usual blunt manner, Isaac came directly to the point. "Well, did you take her, boy?"

Shelah hesitated. He glanced at Tamar. Then, shaking his head, he sighed. "No, but I wish now maybe I had, so he wouldn't be persecuting her like this."

Jacob scratched his beard and spat out a fig seed, which landed near Judah's foot. "Persecuting, huh? What do you mean by that? Isn't your father acting on your behalf in this?"

Shelah tried and failed to fix his father's gaze. Then he turned to Isaac. "No. I told him many moons ago that I had released Tamar to find another husband. He never wanted to give her to me, but he wouldn't release her either."

Jacob's eyes narrowed. "What have you to say to that, Son?"

Judah didn't look up. "I don't have to say anything at all. They never asked for her release until after she had been caught. Then he came to me with this story that he'd released her. It has no meaning. He had no right."

Shelah pushed his father. "You're the one who had no right!"

Judah tossed Shelah to the ground, where he sat staring at his grazed hands.

"Stop it!" Isaac shouted. He waved Carmi away as he sought to explain. "I heard them. The way they've been yelling, old Noah himself could have heard them from his tomb." Extending his hand, he lifted Shelah up. He gentled his voice. "Boy, does she have a husband?"

Shelah grinned. "Yes, Sir. She does."

"What?" Judah looked at Shelah for the first time. "You're lying. You're lying to save her."

Shelah crossed his arms "No, I'm not. She does have a husband."

Isaac intervened. "You know this for a fact?"

"Yes."

"Then name him!" Judah's face was red and angry.

Shelah glanced at Tamar. She turned her face to her father. Shelah smiled as Benu'el nodded, but it quickly faded as Tamar hesitated then shook her head emphatically....no. He sighed. "I can't tell you that. I'm sorry."

Jacob prowled around his son and grandson. "Do you know who the man is, Shelah?"

"Yes, I know." Shelah glared at his father.

"How?"

"Because Enos and Joshua were my witnesses to the taking."

The look on Judah's face must have delighted Jacob, for he danced back to his seat, grabbed another fistful of figs, and took a long swig of wine. "This gets more intriguing all the time. Sit back down, Father Isaac. I want to hear more. Are you saying that you sent these two to witness the marriage...that you knew about it beforehand?"

"Yes, Sir, I did."

"Did you plan it?"

"Yes, Sir."

"Why?"

Shelah again looked to Tamar. Again, she shook her head. "I can't tell you. I wish I could."

Jacob's face colored. He looked around. "Are those witnesses here?"

"Yes, Sir, we are." Enos and Joshua spoke in unison as they made their way forward from opposite sides of the fire.

Jacob approached them. "Does the lad speak the truth? Were you witnesses to a taking?"

Enos replied in his soft Eastern voice, and Joshua's gruff assent chimed in.

Jacob turned first to the slave. "Tell me his name."

"I cannot, Sir. My first obedience is to my young Master, and he forbids it."

"I am your Master," Judah thundered, "and I gave no such command."

"No, Sir. However, long ago you told me my first duty was ever to your son, and while he was a child to guide him, but when he became a man to obey him without fail. I have never disobeyed that instruction."

"Well, I'm changing that instruction right now. Answer the question!"

Enos glanced at Shelah. Shelah shrugged. Enos pursed his lips. "No, Sir, I cannot."

Judah lifted his hand, but Jacob stayed it. "What about you, Joshua? Are you going to talk to us?"

Joshua bowed his head and ran his fingers through his hair. "As Yah lives, Sir, I wish I could."

The back of Judah's hand lashed across Joshua's face and red streaks appeared. "How dare you profane Yah's name with your lies? I'll have your corpse beside hers."

Judah turned to face Father Jacob. "In all truth, it's probably this one who fathered the child in the first place, and he lies to cover his sin."

Drawing his blade, Judah plunged toward Joshua, but Shelah, Enos, and Jacob pulled him back. Even so, Joshua's tunic was torn and his skin bloodied.

Jacob shook Judah by the shoulders. "Judah, cease your ranting now. Two witnesses say the woman has a husband. The case is settled. She is cleared."

A dazed Joshua was pulled out of reach, and Judah attempted to regain his calm, but without much success. "By law, these are no witnesses at all. Enos is a foreign-born slave not bound by the laws of Yah. Therefore, his voice has no sound. Moreover, the other has lived in the deserted city of Chezib alone with her and her family for many years and therefore has good reason to lie. It is likely he is as guilty as she is."

"Liar!" Joshua pulled out his own blade and rushed at Judah. He was caught by both arms before he was halfway there. "You fail to tell them that her family is also my family. Her sister is my wife, and he who offends her honor offends mine. If it is blood you want, Judah of Hebron, you shall have much of it. Yours will soon stain my blade."

Elbowing his captors, he escaped them and charged. The crowd cheered for the combatants. No one could hear Tamar screaming for them to stop. Even Jacob and Isaac's command for them to cease the battle met with no success. They were past reason. Tamar crumpled to the ground. Emi and Ruah rushed to her, shouting for help. This distracted Judah and

Joshua long enough to regain their senses and warily back away from each other.

With the aid of the two slaves who had accompanied them down the hill, Ruah and Emi carried Tamar back up the hill toward her tent. They had not gotten very far when Jacob's voice echoed across the assembly.

"Everyone return to your tents until sundown. My son has spoken the law. Since there are no valid witnesses, unless a husband comes forth to claim her, as the sun goes down to its rest, she will ascend to Yah for His judgment."

Rocking Tamar back and forth, Emi rubbed her with the wet cloth, "Oh, why'd you do it, child? Old Benu'el gave you a nod. I saw him. Why'd you keep quiet like that? You could've ended it."

"Stop rocking, Emi, I'm dizzy enough already." She sat up.

"Well, you're awake now. Answer me."

"I don't know why…It's just…I just…I couldn't embarrass him like that in front of his father. He'd never forgive me."

Emi's jaw dropped open. "Embarrass him. Forgive you. Child, in less time than it takes an old man to walk around the town wall that man is going to strip you naked and set fire to you with your own robes. Don't talk to me about embarrassing him. I'm talking about your life, and you're talking foolishness."

Tamar hugged her. "It isn't foolishness, Emi. Judah is a proud man. It's important.

"Important enough to die for?"

She shrugged. "I hope I don't have to find out."

"Let me take them to him." Ruah squeezed Tamar's hands. "I can get through the guards. Please, I need to do this for you."

Weakly, Tamar nodded and lay back. The pains were coming again, and she was so tired. Ruah scooped up the tokens and turned to leave.

Emi stood in her way. "Have you completely lost your reason, child? Stop! Those are the only proof you have, and that girl admits she once tried to kill you. What makes you so sure this isn't another one of her schemes?"

Arching her back, Tamar sighed. "I'm sure. Go ahead, Ruah."

Emi reached out to stop her, and then threw up her hands as Ruah passed through the tent flap. "Just tell me why."

"Because Shelah loves her."

Emi stopped pacing and peeped out the tent flap again. "Shouldn't we have heard from her by now? The men are still banking the fire, and sundown is less than a watch away. I don't see any sign of the Master either."

Shelah slid under the tent wall and glanced between them. "He's down in the lower part of the camp talking with my uncles. Have either of you seen Ruah?"

"Haven't you?" Tamar's voice rose an octave.

He shook his head. "Not since midday when she left with you. Why?"

"Only because she left here with the tokens right after we got here, and we haven't seen her since, that's why." Emi resumed her pacing.

"She took the tokens? As Yah lives, why?"

Tamar patted his arm. "She promised to take them to the Master. She probably just wanted to deliver them privately, and she hasn't had a chance." At least, she hoped that was all there was to it.

Emi scoffed. "More likely she threw them in a fire and ran as far away as she could get."

"No." Shelah shook his head. "She wouldn't do that."

"Tell me then, why not? Ruah hated Tamar. She admitted it."

Shelah patted Emi's shoulder. "That was a long time ago. Besides, she loves me, Emi, and she wouldn't do anything to risk losing me."

Emi grunted. "You've got a high opinion of yourself. Hate's a powerful force. Makes many forget everything else."

"No, she wouldn't. Especially not now. Love is more powerful than hate. Tamar is proof of that."

Tamar waved Emi's retort away. "What's so special about now?"

Shelah grinned. "We're going to have a babe. She just told me."

"That's wonderful." Tamar hugged him.

"Are you certain you're not the father, boy?" Jacob boomed as he stepped into the tent. "Look pretty friendly to me."

Shelah laughed. "No, Sir, not of this child anyway. I was just telling Tamar that my wife Ruah and I are going to have a babe. We were married last fall at the barley feast."

Jacob gathered his rich robes around him and squatted down next to the clay lamp. "I see. Now, young woman, has your husband come forward yet?"

She shook her head.

"Would you care to name him for me now that we're alone?"

"No, Sir." Her voice was soft.

He stood. "Then you leave me no choice. Come with me. Preparations are being made, and I assume you would like to see your father one last time."

He turned to leave, but Emi clutched his sleeve. "Look, can't this be put off. At least until the babes are born. I doubt it would be more than another day or two."

He shook his head. "It wouldn't do any good anyway. Without a father to claim them, their cords couldn't be tied. It's the law."

Shelah stepped forward. "What if I claim them? I would put them between my knees and adopt them."

Jacob clapped him to his chest. "You're a good boy, Son. You remind me much of my son Joseph. But you're still a boy.

You go against your father on this, and he'll send you and your wife out on your own. Then what would you do?"

"We'd survive somehow." Shelah squared his shoulders. "Yah would protect us."

"It won't be necessary, Shelah." Tamar took his hand. "Their father will claim them."

She wondered again what was taking Ruah so long. Time was running out.

Judah plunged into the darkness of his tent. Someone had blown out all his lamps. Then he sensed he was not alone. "Who's there? I have no time today for foolishness."

"Good evening, Master." Ruah's voice sounded lightly out of the darkness. "I have been waiting for you for a very long time. Where have you been?"

"With my brothers. What have you done to my lamps?"

She giggled. "Put them out, of course."

He still could not locate her voice. "Are you drunk?"

"No, Master."

"Then why did you put out my lights?"

Her voice was still soft. Perhaps the softness was what made it seem so ominous. "It grows dark here as the grave is dark. Er lies in darkness. Onan lies in darkness. Now you would send the Mistress to lie in darkness also. I thought you should taste of it yourself."

"I have been in the dark many times, Ruah. I am not a child afraid of the night. Don't be ridiculous. Besides, the sun still shines outside. All I have to do is to lift up the tent flap."

She had gotten behind him, and though her voice was still soft, it threatened. "Not yet, Master. I have not finished talking with you yet. The sun will not shine much longer, you know. Then she will die. Shall she lie between Er and Onan, or will that be forbidden her as a harlot?"

Her voice kept moving around. Why had his eyes not grown accustomed to the darkness? "Yes...No...I don't know...Why?"

"Come now, Master. You know everything about the law. About who can be born, and who must die. What they can do. Where they can lie." Another giggle. "Wouldn't Onan be proud of me? I can rhyme. Lie...die...die...lie." Her voice had taken on the songlike quality of Onan's.

"Stop this, Ruah, or I'm leaving."

"No, Master, you're not leaving until I allow it. I will have an answer. Yah is not your God. The law is. Now answer me! Will she lie with Er?"

"No, she will not be buried. Does that give you pleasure? Even in death, she will not take Er from you."

For a time, there was silence. "No, Master," she whispered. "She does not want him. She never did. All this time I accused her wrongly. All she ever wanted was you. You were the guilty one. You still are, but I cannot be your judge. Yah does that quite well."

Judah started to leave but her voice once again halted him. "Tell me, Master. What of the man? He has no bulging belly to give his secret away. Is he any less guilty?"

"No, of course not. Adultery is adultery for both."

"Shall he then be put to death?"

"Now what are you saying, Ruah? Have you lost your senses entirely?"

Throwing up the entire tent flap, she flooded the room with sunlight. "The Mistress sends a message. By the man to whom these belong is she with child." She left him.

There, spread out neatly before him on the black blanket, were his tokens: his shepherd's staff, his crested ring, and his ragged prayer shawl. He fell down on his knees before Yah.

The sun was just touching the peak of the mountain when the crowd reassembled and the flames of lit torches were touched to unlit ones until the firelight spread across the hillside. Old women began the lamentation chant. Its echo chilled Emi's bones.

The Old Master Jacob was still taking charge. *Enjoying himself, too.* He did seem concerned for the child though. Maybe he didn't believe her guilty. She grunted and muttered, "More likely he likes to spite his son."

Jacob's apparent sympathy didn't change the fact they had taken Tamar away and bound her by the wrists and feet like a sacrificial lamb. Emi tried to go to her, but two guards held her back.

Where is that slave girl? The child usually had such good instincts about people. But love made you see things different. She sure hoped they could trust her. *Huh, there she comes, throwing herself at the Young Master, kissing him in front of all these folks. That was the problem with young folks. They've got no shame.*

Jacob raised his arms and announced in a loud voice. "I'm afraid my son could not face the end of this tragedy; however, the time has come." He turned to Tamar. "Young woman, have you anything to say before you face the throne of Yah's judgment?"

Her eyes were glazed, and Emi feared she was taking one of her spells, but finally she shook her head emphatically.

"Strip her." Jacob turned to pick up one of the torches.

"No! Stop!" Even as the servant cut the jeweled band that held her tunic, the Master's voice sounded from the back edge of the crowd. A path cleared for him.

"Ah, you came after all. Sorry we didn't wait. I thought maybe your bowels weren't strong enough to take what your heart demanded. Well, you're here now. Let's get this over with." Jacob nodded to the slave.

"I said no. Stop."

Jacob shrugged and motioned the slave away. "Now tell me why."

"She's innocent."

"I see. Now she's innocent."

"Yes. Cut her loose."

"Why?"

"Shelah spoke the truth. She has a husband."

"Oh, and do you also refuse to tell us his name?"

Judah pulled out his blade and slit Tamar's bonds. Turning to his father, he held her to himself. "I do not refuse. His name is Judah of Hebron, son of Jacob."

Whatever the Old Master might have expected, it wasn't this. He gaped at them wide-eyed. "Is this some new ploy? Have you too lost your senses? You are the one who wanted her burned."

Judah laughed. "No, Father. I've not lost my senses. It seems I've finally found them."

Jacob called for his cushions. "Then would you kindly explain this whole situation to me? I'm mystified."

"Actually, there's very little to explain. It seems, like my father, I've been deceived by a very crafty woman, and by my own son. She was disguised at the time, and although I found myself fascinated by her, I did not recognize her. I even saw the two witnesses on the hillside, though of course it never occurred to me at the time that they were witnesses to a taking. I saw them simply as guards to a prostitute. It was only just now that I found out that it was me she shielded."

Jacob waved him to continue, so he lifted her into his arms and spoke more to her than to the assembled group. "Long ago I promised myself to her in marriage, but almost before that promise was out of my mouth, I broke it. I had vowed never to have but one wife simply out of jealousy for the love that you bore for Rachel instead of my mother. Therefore, I gave Tamar instead to Er. Even after Er and Onan died, I sent her back to her father to await Shelah's coming of age. That time came and passed. I couldn't give her away again. I told myself it was for Shelah's safety, but it was pure jealousy. I am a jealous man. When I was told she was to have a child, grew enraged and called this council together. Anger filled me at what seemed infidelity, not to Shelah, but to me. It was not true. She is far more righteous than I can ever hope to be. If anyone should be burned here today, let it be me."

As he finished speaking, Tamar buried her face in his chest and wept.

"For what?" Jacob laughed. "Unless you can tell me otherwise, there's no law against a man taking a bride. Now let's go home."

"Wait, Father. I have more to confess...to you...about Joseph."

Tears gleamed in the Old Master's eyes. "There's no need, Son. I've known for years, but I'm proud that you have finally become man enough to admit it."

"No, you don't understand. We didn't kill him..."

"No, you sold him to traders headed for Egypt."

Judah gasped. "You've known?"

Jacob clasped him on the shoulder. "Go home with your wife, Son. She needs you."

Judah insisted on carrying her all the way back to the tent, and she felt so content in his arms. It was as though all the years had been wiped away.

"We have so much time to make up for." He kissed the tip of her nose as he laid her back on the cushion.

"Well, you're not going to start now." Emi entered the tent behind them. "That child's going to drop those babes any minute, and you're not going to speed them up with your foolishness."

"But it's not time yet." Judah's brow wrinkled.

"Don't matter. Babes come when they please, and when there's two of them, they seldom hold the full time." She tapped his shoulder vigorously. "If you're getting suspicious again, I swear I'll take my cooking pot to the top of your head."

Wincing under the pressure of her bony finger, he threw up his hands. "I swear before Yah, I had no such thought. I was worried, that's all."

"Well you'd better not. Or you'll answer to me this time."

"I won't. I promise. Leave me a remnant of my shoulder, please."

Emi withdrew her finger. "I'm sorry, Master. I forgot myself."

"You're forgiven." He laid his hand on Tamar's belly, and then his ear to hear the strong heartbeats. "Just tell me the babes are in no danger."

Emi wiped her hands on her tunic. "They'll make it. After all this, they're still kicking hard. They'll make it."

She seemed sincere about the babes, but Tamar had known her all her life, and one thing was clear to her. Emi was worried. If not about the babes…

Chapter 11

Tamar gripped Emi's shoulders as she straddled the wooden birthing stool. Pain reddened her face as she fought the desire to push. At least she had delivered so many babes that Emi's instructions were a comfort. It was much harder from this side though.

"Grit your teeth and hold on tight, child. Don't push yet. One of them has his hand stuck out, and I need to bind it with a piece of thread so we'll know it's the oldest. That's it. Grunt. Yell if you want to. There now, it's on. Wait, he pulled his hand back in. Here he comes. Why, bless me. It's not the same one. See, no thread. He's a boy. Big one too for someone built as tiny as you. Ruah, run him outside to the Master so he can tie his cord and bind him up. And be sure to tell him about the scarlet thread."

"Yes ma'am." Ruah took the squealing bundle and held his cord high above her head. "He's a beautiful babe, Mistress. The Master will be proud."

Emi grunted. "You tell him I said pride is a sin."

"You tell me, Emi." Judah entered the tent and placed a kiss on her weathered cheek. "I'll take him, Ruah. You get back over there and help the Mistress."

"Don't you know this is women's work? What are you doing here? You'd best go back outside now." Emi turned her back on Judah.

"By what law?" He expertly tied the cord, passed his sharp blade across the fire, and in one motion cut off the excess cord. "Hi, dearest, are you all right?"

Tamar nodded.

Emi sighed. "My law, only I'll make an exception this time, but only because you being here seems to have already calmed her a bit. Mind you, don't you get any fancy notions I'm afraid of you. And don't talk to her too much. She's got other things on her mind right now."

"How would I get a silly notion like that, Emi? My shoulder still aches." He kissed Tamar's cheek. "Have you named him yet?"

"I said don't talk to her!"

"Oh, Emi, I'm fine. Let me talk." But she had to stop a moment and breathe deeply before she could continue. "Not yet. An odd thing happened though that we might want to think about." Another breath. "A hand popped out and Emi put a scarlet thread on it. Then this one came out with no scarlet thread."

Judah laughed. "I see. Then we should call him Perez because he overtook his brother."

She nodded approval then grunted for another birth pain. "How do you know it's another brother?"

"I don't."

"Well you soon will, Master. Here it comes!" Emi pushed Judah aside.

"Is it a boy?"

"That isn't the end you can tell from. Now, back away. Ruah, get me some more towels. These babes are splitting her like lightening splits a palm tree." The shoulder broke through, and the tiny fist with the scarlet thread appeared. "All right, Master, place that one to her breast and be ready to take this one. Here he comes. It's another boy. Watch it, he's a bit slippery."

Judah laughed again. "His color is good, Emi, and look at all that hair. I think it's going to be red like Father's. He'll love that."

Tears blurred Tamar's vision and she laughed as she wiped them. "It is bright."

Passing the knife through the fire again, he tied and cut the cord. "Get me the bindings, Ruah. I think we should name him Zerah. 'Brightness,' that he may forever stand in the bright light of Yah's truth."

Placing Zerah at her other breast, he picked up the still-suckling Perez. "I'd best find a slave to be a wet-nurse."

Perez found his finger and suckled it. "I think maybe we'll need a couple for these two. Especially this one. I fear he's going to be quite the Proud Prince."

"Just like his father." Emi nodded.

Judah and Tamar sat together in the tent. The flap was up to give the sleeping babes the breeze before the setting sun, at least what little there might be of it.

Only a handful of days had passed since the trial, but already she felt as comfortable with him as if they had never spent the years apart. "Do you really have to go?"

He stroked her hair, and laid a little kiss on each eyelid. "I'm afraid so, Little One. You've charmed Father so much that he has finally consented to let us take Benjamin with us, and we can't afford to give him time to change his mind."

He moved to stir the half-filled lentil pot simmering in the middle of the tent. "Food is getting too scarce, and that Minister warned us not to come back without Ben. But I'll get back as soon as I possibly can. I promise."

"I wonder why?" She took the paddle from him.

"Because I'll miss you," he whispered. "Don't you know that yet?"

She laughed and kissed him lightly. "No, I meant I wondered why he wanted you to bring Ben." She ladled out a serving of the beans for him and urged him to sit.

He lay back and rested on his elbow. "I've been wondering the same thing for all these years now, and I still can't figure it out."

"Tell me again about this Minister. What did he look like?"

As he ate, Judah explained to her all about the strange first meeting with the Minister of Pharaoh. "What does it matter what he looks like? He's handsome enough, I suppose."

She shrugged. "I don't know. I just have a feeling it's important."

"It's important that he's handsome?" He laughed. "Are you planning to replace me already?"

"If you're going to leave me, don't waste time teasing me." She planted kisses on his eyelids. "Just hold me for a while."

They sat together until Emi finally came in to tell him his caravan was waiting.

The first of the donkeys was already disappearing over the horizon. Judah had held his animals back to the very end so that he might spend more time with Tamar. She thought she could just make out his form at the base of the mountain. The reddish hue of the sunset was quickly turning to purple. Soon darkness would blanket the sky, and the sliver of the new moon with its myriad of stars would take its place.

Emi's wrinkled hand rested heavily on her shoulder.

"I'm never going to be with him again, am I, Emi?"

Emi wiped the tears from her cheeks, and handed her a rough cloth. For a time she didn't answer, just stood beside her staring at the fading caravan.

Finally she whispered, "I just don't know for sure, but I don't think so, child. Those babes tore you up pretty bad, and you're not healing at all like you should. I'm afraid your blood's turned on you."

Kneeling, she clasped Tamar's cold hands in her warm one. "I'm afraid Yah's all out of miracles for you two."

"No." Tamar shook her head. "Don't ever believe that, Emi. There's a whole land of miracles on the other side of that mountain. Yah's still there, Emi. He still cares."

Infant cries pierced the air, and together they entered the tent.

THE END

Share It
If you enjoyed "Tokens of Promise," I would appreciate it if you would help others enjoy this book too.
Recommend it. Please help other readers find this book by recommending it to friends, readers' groups and discussion boards.
Review it. Please tell other readers why you liked this book by reviewing it at one of the following websites: Amazon, Barnes and Noble, or Goodreads.

If you do write a review, please email the link of your review to reviews@hopespringsbooks.com and you will be entered in a drawing to receive a free copy of HopeSpring's next book as a way of thanking you.

GLOSSARY

Abba : Father
Ephah : Dry measure equivalent to a bushel
Go'el : Redeemer
Habiri : ancient tribe of Abraham
HaSatan : The Satan or Serpent
Hierodule : Temple prostitute or priestess
Mitzvah : good deed
Qaseh : Another word for Hierodule
Qerah : piece, rag
Samael : Satan's chief demon
Zonah : Common prostitute

AUTHOR'S NOTES

The first time I read the story of Tamar in Genesis 38, it popped off the page at me like an errant Jack-in-the-box. A friend had given me a grocery bag full of Harlequin romances, and this read just like one of them. I was convinced this was the love story of Tamar and Judah. But more than that it was the story of a woman in a culture entirely dominated by men, who nevertheless consciously decided not to be a victim anymore, and took charge to fulfill the destiny she believed the Lord had ordained for her.

In addition, it seemed to me that the story had a point that had been completely overlooked by most of the scholarship I read at the time. The Judah of Genesis chapter 42 is hardly recognizable as the same man seen in chapter 37. He who earlier sold one brother into slavery offers up his own life to save another. The story of Tamar is the only event recorded to account for the difference. In New Testament phraseology, it would simply have to be termed a "conversion experience." Perhaps the overt sexuality of the passage blinds us to this, but we cannot deny that Judah is one who somehow learns that his outward appearance of righteousness is truly as "filthy rags" and faith becomes his only hope.

The first step of my writing was to immerse myself in the ancient culture as much as possible. I read as many books on the subject as I could find. Among these were: <u>Ancient Israel</u>, <u>Old Testament World,</u> and <u>Everyday Life in Old Testament Times</u>. I also attempted to make mental pictures of specific scenes of home life in a Patriarchal camp. There are no pictures or engravings of people or places native to the culture. Only a few stylistic drawings of Egyptian or Mesopotamian origin give any clue to Hebrew appearance. Pictures of modern Bedouin life in the Middle East became my only resource for this exercise. These can be found in National Geographic's <u>Everyday Life in Bible Times</u>. Also helpful was a PBS series entitled, *Heritage—the Civilization of the Jews.*

One of the first major obstacles I encountered was the Name of God. I learned that Jehovah is a 14th century misnomer, and that Yahweh would be offensive to some Jewish readers. Adonai (lord, master), Elohim (god, non-specific), and El Shaddai (God of Might) were all possibilities, but somehow didn't seem quite right. I tried LORD and LORD God, but these were considered too distracting. After a lot of deliberation, I decided, (although still with some reservations) on Yah. Many scholars believe it to be one of the earliest names of God: hence "Hallelujah" (praise Yah) and the name Jonathan (Yah given), but a few scholars believe it to refer to another god entirely.

Another problem was the language. I wanted it to be modern enough to be easily readable, but in the rhythm and style of the Hebrew and without anachronisms. I also wanted Judah and Tamar's speech to be slightly formal while that of Er, Emi and Ruah was much more colloquial. Onan's speech had to be bizarre because he suffered many symptoms of schizophrenia as well as learning disorders.

Another linguistic difficulty was the expression of measurements. Time wasn't divided into minutes and hours in ancient Israel, but by physically observable occurrences like "the breeze before the setting sun." The seven-day week with the Sabbath set aside as a day of rest was a uniquely Jewish invention, however, many scholars agree that the days were originally reckoned from morning to morning instead of sunset to sunset as is the present Jewish tradition. Therefore, when Judah wanted to leave Chezib, he was considering the distance he could travel before the dawn.

Likewise metrology was empirically determined: a "cubit" was the distance from the elbow to the tip of the middle finger of an adult male, a "span" was from the tip of the thumb to the tip of the little finger with the fingers outspread; an "homer", an ass-load, etc. Most trading was done in the bartering of goods. When money was used, it was weighed, not counted, with the shekel as the basic unit of measurement.

The major source of the story is, of course, the Bible, especially focusing on Genesis 38 but also including many of the earlier stories of the Patriarchs. To supplement these, I used both Rabbinic and scholarly commentary on Genesis. The legends of Tamar can be found in <u>HaAggadah,</u> and the <u>Mishnah</u> and <u>Halakah</u> include commentary on the Levirite marriage laws as well as discussions of the sins of Er and Onan. <u>The Journal of Biblical Literature</u> is one source of scholarly comment. The tale Judah tells in chapter eleven is from Jewish folklore found in <u>The Lore of the Old Testament.</u>

We must realize that much of the Biblical account of Tamar, as well as my story, is based on laws that will not actually be written until four hundred years after the patriarchal period when Moses is given the law on Mt. Sinai. However, the concept of an earlier oral tradition is widely accepted.

I have placed a great deal of emphasis on shoes in the first few chapters for several reasons. First, according to tradition, money from the sale of Joseph was used to buy shoes. This is consistent with Jewish law in that money from the sale of a slave could not be used to buy food or for tithing, but it could be used for clothing, or more often to buy shoes. Second, in traditional symbolism, broken shoes are an overt sexual image. In a more general sense, they are the casting off of inhibitions and traditional restraints. However, in Biblical literature, they have a more important function. Bare feet are directly connected to poverty; hence to ritual poverty, and paradoxically to holiness. Thus, Moses was commanded to take off his shoes because he was standing on holy ground. The meeting between Tamar and Judah should therefore be seen as a divine encounter.

The subject matter of this story is frankly sexual in nature, and I don't apologize for that. The Bible was not ashamed to tell it. The narrative is not meant to be a graphic depiction of the sexual perversions of the ancient people. It is, however, important to see that one's sexuality and one's religion were so tightly bound in that society that you cannot talk about one without the other. Unfortunately, in our society, Christians have decided not to talk about such "worldly" matters as sex, and thus we have blindly handed the entire realm of sexuality over to Satan.

The sin Er commits in the story is the one he is accused of in the Talmud. Although the sin of Onan has traditionally been thought of as "Onanism" or masturbation, many scholars now reject this in favor of "coitus interruptus". I kept the traditional definition but extended it to ritual castration because of the connection scholars make between Tamar and Astarte. Part of the ritual worship of Astarte was castration by her priests who then placed their organs on her altar as a sacrifice. Although some scholars agree that the real sin of Onan was idolatry of the beauty of Tamar, this interpretation of the "spilling of his seed" is entirely my own invention. Genesis does make a fine distinction in that it says that Er himself "was wicked and the Lord slew him," but that "the thing which he [Onan] did was wicked and the Lord slew him also." This was my ground for making Onan mentally disturbed and therefore not responsible for his actions.

The worship of Astarte and Tamar as a hierodule (qaseh) are linked together. A hierodule is a temple priestess, usually in the temple of Astarte or Baal. Though allowed to be married, they are not allowed to bear children to mortals; therefore, they engage in profane sexual practices. They remain veiled in the presence of even the men of their own family. Because Judah didn't recognize Tamar at Enaim, scholars assume she had worn a veil around him all that time, so she must have been a hierodule. A "zonah," or common prostitute, was forbidden to wear a veil in public, and Judah going to a hierodule seems unbelievable.

There was no wedding in the modern sense in ancient Israel. The sex act itself was the marriage ceremony. However, the taking of a bride was a public act with witnesses to examine the "tokens of virginity". They could then swear, if necessary, that the bride was truly a "virgin of Israel". Our conception of marriage in Biblical times is limited especially in that we find it hard to contemplate marriage at the onset of puberty.

It wasn't until I really began to study the Hebrew meaning of words that I began to see all the Messianic symbolism in this story. I really wish the Bible code people would get hold of it and examine it closely. Shelah means "Righteous one" and "trickster." How can someone be both righteous and a trickster? Matthew 10:16 tells us to be as "shrewd as serpents and innocent as doves." Shelah has to have been in on the trick. Otherwise, Tamar would be just as guilty as Judah.

Enaim is the "place of the opening of eyes." In the Garden of Eden, Satan told Eve sin would open her eyes and make her wise, but he lied. Sin closes our eye to God's truth. Only confession and redemption can open them again.

Tamar received three tokens from Judah: his seal ring: a symbol of economic wealth; his cord (the Hebrew word is that of the corded edge of the prayer shawl); and his shepherd's staff. Jesus received three gifts from the wise men: gold, a symbol of economic wealth, frankincense (a symbol of his priestly function), and myrrh (a symbol of his death as the Lamb of God). Tamar even sat at the crossroads or gateway to Enaim, in Hebrew the "eye." Can we not see the symbolism here?

Modern scholars insist that Tamar was a pagan who had some faint knowledge that Jewish men treated women better than did their neighbors. According to the Talmud, she was a "prophetess, a righteous daughter of Shem." Like Job, there were other Yahweh worshippers in ancient Israel. Judah says that "she is more righteous than I." These are exactly the same words that Saul says of King David. Why do modern scholars reject them, and continue to portray her as a pagan? Because they refuse to believe that God would tell her to sit at a crossroad and pretend to be a prostitute, that's why. Yet, God rewards this very act with a child who is part of the lineage of Christ. There is no way this could be anything other than His plan. He would not have rewarded it otherwise.

The name Tamar means palm tree: the kind that often splits into two trees. Tamar's two sons represent two righteous branches: Perez, the child of the covenant, the Jewish people; and Zerah, the child of the scarlet thread, the church. Tamar is from a village named Chezib that is also called Achzib, which means "deceptive" or "failing." In Micah 1:14, the reference to Chezib suggests that the town name is related to a winter brook, which failed in the summer.

Romans 11:10 and 25 tell us that God closed the eyes of the Jewish people to the truth of their Messiah until the time of the Gentiles has passed. With the rapture of His church, our time will end, and that time is rapidly approaching. My prayer is that this work will cause Christians and Jews to open their eyes and see our Messiah written in this Old Testament story of the redemption of Judah.

God bless you,

Teresa Pollard

DISCUSSION GUIDE

BOOK ONE
Chapter One
1. What do wells symbolize? (John 4:6, Ex. 2:15, Song 4:15)
2. What does a broken shoe symbolize? (Deut. 29:5, Is. 20:2, Josh. 5:15)
3. Why was Tamar subject to stoning? (Lev.18, Lam. 1:8)
4. If Benu'el were truly a prophet, why would he give Tamar to a man like Ben Qara? (Ex. 19:5)
5. Is love an act of the will? Is lust? Why or why not? How should we react to such feelings? (Gal. 5:16-25, 1 John 2:16-24)

Chapter Two
1. Judah vowed never to have but one wife. Had he already broken that vow? (Matt. 5:28)
2. What was the significance to Judah of the striped cloth? (Gen. 37:3)
3. In a drunken stupor, Judah had married Ashuah. Now he caught himself repeating that same scenario. What role do alcohol and drugs play in sinful acts? (Prov. 20:1)
4. Although this story takes place long before Moses received the law on Mt. Sinai, it is generally accepted that there was an oral tradition of laws from early on. In what way did Judah keep the law? How did he break it? (Ex 20:8, Rom. 12:13)

Chapter Three

1. Abraham came from Ur, which is in Sumer, the birthplace of our alphabet. Surely, this is no coincidence. Judah is fascinated by the art of writing, which we take for granted. Do you have a family story you should pass down to your children? Your own testimony? Have you done so? Why not write it now?

2. Why did Judah confess to Tamar? Why didn't she believe him? Was she seeing him as he was or through rose colored glasses? Or is the truth somewhere in between?

3. Judah called Tamar his wife. He also uncovered her. Obviously, he wanted her. It was legal to have two wives. Why would he then announce she was to marry Er? (Gen. 29:20-30)

4. How was slavery different in ancient Israel from other countries? What is a bond slave? (Lev.25:39-, Ex. 21:1-6)

Chapter Four

1. What is prayer? What does Scripture teach about it? (Luke 11:1-13, Matt. 23:23, Phil. 4:6).

2. Archaeologists tell us this time was the beginning of iron instruments for cooking and tools. Imagine the difference between cooking food in the dirt and on a grill. How might this have changed life?

3. Is it ever too late to change? If you could change something in your life, what would it be? How could you change it?

4. Why did Er want to keep his relationship with Ruah secret? What does the Bible say about secret sin? (Ps.69:5, Mark 4:22)

5. Tamar was angry with God. Have you ever felt that way? How did you deal with it? Is being angry a sin? (Eph. 4:26)

Chapter Six
1. Why does God care about our sexual practices? (1 Cor. 6:19, Rom.12:1)
2. Did Er have a right to be angry? How might he have handled his anger without sin?
3. How might Ruah have put an end to Er's physical and sexual abuse before it escalated? What could she have done even afterwards? Why didn't she?
4. Why do so many rape victims cover up the rape? Are we somehow conditioned as children to think that "tattling" is the worst sin a person can commit?
5. Do you think Ashuah suspected the truth? Why would she not say anything?

Chapter Seven
1. Why does God allow evil?
2. How did ancient wedding customs differ from ours? Are there any ways they are alike?

Chapter Eight
1. Psychologists say we are a product of nature and nurture, yet two children can be born of the same parents and raised in the same environment, yet one is good and the other evil. Why is this possible? (Rom. 8:29)
2. How is Judah's response to his anger different from Er's?
3. What was the Old Testament penalty for striking your parent? For cursing them? (Ex. 21:15, 17)

4. The Bible says Er was evil and the Lord slew him. Why does it seem sometimes as if God allows some evil people to live for so long, yet takes other good people at a very young age?

Chapter Nine

1. What did tearing your clothes symbolize? Is it a coincidence that when Jesus died the temple veil tore from top to bottom? What did that mean? (Luke 23:45)
2. What was the test of a true prophet (or prophetess)? (Deut. 18:22)
3. God has promised that all things work together to those who love him and are called according to His purpose (Rom. 8:28). How is this possible? How has this proved true in your life?
4. Have you ever faced a situation where what seemed right for one person would hurt another? How should we respond to such situations? (Rom. 8:26)
5. Why was Ruah not legally Er's wife? Why would they allow an innocent child to pay the price for their sin? Did the Old Testament actually command this? (Deut. 23:2)

Chapter Ten

1. Why did God create sex? (Gen. 2:23-24, 3:16, 18:12, Heb. 13:4)
2. The Israelites took the command against graven images as a command against all art. Why would God make such a command, or did He? (Ex. 20:5). What should be our response to the work of our hands?
3. Why would Judah have told Ashuah of Ruah's accusations? Is it possible he really did love her?

Chapter Eleven

1. As written in this story, do you think Onan was responsible for his actions? Why or why not?
2. What is Ruah's responsibility for the ensuing tragedy? When are we responsible for other people twisting our words? When are we not responsible for it?
3. The story Judah tells is an ancient Jewish legend. How do such stories provide a link to our own cultural history? Why is this important?
4. Obviously Onan wasn't ready for marriage, but would he ever have been? Why or why not?

Chapter Twelve

1. What is the best way to deal with fear? (1 John 4:18, Ps. 23:4, Ps. 27:1, Matt. 10:26).
2. The sin Onan commits in this chapter is actually the sin the Talmud accuses him of. What is it?

Chapter Thirteen

1. Tamar says, "Sometimes the ways of Yah cannot be understood by His children; they are only meant to be obeyed." Do you agree with this statement? Why or why not?
2. Why did Onan believe Tamar to be Astarte? Who did he believe himself to be? What commandment did he break here? (Ex. 20:3-5) Note: Most scholars (both ancient and modern) agree that idolatry was the real sin of Onan since it was his motive for whatever he did.

3. What dream did Joseph have that this situation reminded Judah of? (Gen. 37:9-11) What did that dream mean?

Chapter Fourteen
1. As parents, how responsible are we for the actions of our children? How can we respond when we have tried our best to "raise them up in the nurture and admonition of the Lord", but they choose evil instead?
2. What excuse did Ashuah use to shift the blame to Tamar for Onan's actions? Is that a typical motherly reaction? Is it wrong to think the best of our children? Can that become idolatry? How do we avoid that trap?
3. Was Judah wrong to give in to Ashuah's demand that Tamar leave? What, if anything, could he have done differently?
4. Hirah says, "I respect your God because He is your God, but I will gladly be unclean if I can comfort my friend." Did he actually have a better understanding of godliness than Judah did?

BOOK TWO
Chapter One
1. How had the town changed since Judah's visit? How should the Christian respond to a poor economy? (2 Chron. 7:14)
2. Why do you think Shelah mentioned his brothers' names? He said the mention of their names brought God like a shield around her. (2 Sam. 22:31) Have you ever felt like God was a shield around you in a situation? How did you respond?

Chapter Two

1. Benu'el feels satisfaction that Judah has suffered. That is a natural human, but not necessarily godly, reaction. Even as Christians, we sometimes feel ungodly emotions. How should we deal with those? (1 John 1:9, Matt. 5:44).
2. How did Benu'el's pride contribute to Tamar's suffering? In trying to protect our loved ones, how do we sometimes contribute to their pain?
3. Discuss the difference between Judah's, Er's and Shelah's concept of a "man of leisure." What does it mean to you?
4. Benu'el gives his mantle to Shelah. What does that signify? (2 Kings 2:13).
5. What is the symbolism of shaking out your shoe? (Ruth 4:7).

Chapter Three

1. Judah thinks it ironic that of all the terrible things he has done in his life, he is jailed for trying to save lives. Have you ever felt like that; that you were being persecuted for trying to help someone? What does Christ say about that? (Matt. 10:42, 1 Pet. 4:14-19).
2. Why do you think the brothers didn't recognize Joseph? Why did Joseph put the money back in their sacks?
3. What was the relationship between Jacob and Judah like? Why? Has your relationship to your parents or your children ever been strained? How was it healed?
4. What is generational sin? Have you felt the effects of it? How can we break the cycle? (Deut. 5:9).

5. Shelah says his father did the right thing for the wrong reasons. Why does God care about our motives as long as we do the right thing?

Chapter Four
1. Shelah says Ruah has changed. How is that possible? Have you ever known someone who dramatically changed? How did you know it was real?
2. Judah's concern was for feeding his people, a worthy goal. He contemplated playing a trick on Joseph. Why didn't he? Does the end ever justify the means? Why or why not?
3. Describe the character of Shelah. Was he "soft?" Why do we tend to equate "manliness" with "roughness?" How can a man be both extremely gentle and "manly?"

Chapter Five
1. What was the difference between a "zonah" (common prostitute) and a "hierodule" (temple prostitute)? Why is the distinction important here?
2. Why was it important to get tokens of Judah's identity?
3. When Tamar innocently flirts with Joshua, his reaction is intense. How are men programmed differently sexually than women? What is a woman's responsibility to that knowledge?

Chapter Six
1. What is the symbolism of a shepherd's staff? (John 1:29, 10:11)
2. What is the symbolism of a gold signet ring? (Dan. 6:17)

3. What is the symbolism of the cord? (The word in Hebrew is that of the corded edge of a prayer shawl or tallith.) (Ex. 39:21)
4. How do these compare to the gifts that Jesus received from the wise men? (Gold, frankincense (Ex. 30:34), and myrrh (Luke 23:56, John 19:40)) What does this say to you about Tamar's trick? Why?

Chapter Seven
1. Ruah tells Shelah about Tamar's pregnancy and listens to his conversation with Hirah. Even as Christians, do we sometimes find it easy to fall back into the same old sins? How should we respond to those urges? (Jam. 4:7-8, 1 John 1:9)

Chapter Eight
1. Why was Judah so upset that Tamar was pregnant? Why did he have any right to condemn her if Shelah did not?
2. Why would Tamar be burned instead of stoned? (Lev. 21:9).

Chapter Nine
1. Benu'el said, "The time is not yet ripe." How can we know whether something is God's timing or our timing?

Chapter Ten
1. Emi says the people need someone to blame for the drought, and Tamar is it. How do we find scapegoats for our troubles even today? What are some examples?
2. What is the significance of two witnesses? (Deut. 17:6, 19:15)

3. What was Judah's response to seeing the tokens? What should be our response when confronted with our own sin? (Acts 17:30-31).

4. How did Judah's confession lead to healing with his father?

Chapter Eleven

1. What is the significance of the scarlet thread? (Josh. 2:18, Matt. 27:28)

2. What does the name Perez mean? What does Zerah mean? Does your name mean anything? How does it describe you?

3. What did Judah find when he returned to Egypt? (See Gen. 43-50)

4. How is the Judah of chapter 43 changed from the Judah of chapter 37? What is the only story given to account for this redemption of Judah? (Gen. 37:26, 43:8-9)

5. Unfortunately, "God told me to do it" has been used as an excuse to justify all kinds of evil through the ages. Why is this never a valid excuse? (1 Timothy 3:16, Heb. 1:1-3, John 16:13-14)

ABOUT THE AUTHOR

Teresa Pollard is from Richmond, Virginia, and was saved at a young age. She has a Masters degree in English and Creative Writing from Hollins College, and has served as a Sunday School teacher and children's worker for most of the last forty years. Married for forty years, she was devastated by divorce and the death of her youngest daughter, but God has blessed her with a new home and another grandson, and she now resides in Dacula, Georgia.

Her website is www.TeresaPollardWrites.com

HopeSprings Books has also published "Not Guilty" by Teresa Pollard and Candi Pullen.